TOPLINERS

GENERAL EDITOR: AIDA

Sell-Out

*So that night I went round the streets smashing gaslamps
... You would do the same if you were twelve and your
mother told you what my mother told me.*

Danny Rowley feels desperately that his mother should
not marry again. His dad is dead but no one can replace
him. His struggles against this situation involve Danny
in increasing rows and troubles; with his family, a rival
gang and the police.

TOPLINERS

Sell-Out

Reginald Maddock

Macmillan

First published by Collins 1969
This edition first published 1972
Reprinted 1973, 1975, 1977, 1979 (twice), 1981, 1982

Published by
MACMILLAN EDUCATION LTD
*Houndmills Basingstoke Hampshire RG21 2XS
and London
Associated companies in Delhi Dublin
Hong Kong Johannesburg Lagos Melbourne
New York Singapore and Tokyo*

Printed in Hong Kong

Contents

1 Vandal

So that night I went round the streets smashing gas-lamps. I wouldn't do it now, but then, when I was only twelve, I did it. You would do the same if you were twelve and your mother told you what my mother told me.

'It'll be nice for you, Danny,' she said. 'Better than it's been for the past couple of years. You're a big boy and you need a man.'

I listened, trying not to believe, hating her words as they hung in the air, shutting them out of my ears yet hearing them ring in my head, until I wanted to die.

'You need somebody to help you with your home-work,' she said. 'It's getting beyond me.'

My insides had twisted into knots and I wanted to cry, to stamp, to scream, but twelve's too old for crying and stamping and screaming.

'You need a father,' she said.

'*I had one!*'

I hurled the words at her like rocks and she staggered back.

'Danny...' she whispered, but I rushed out of the house and through Benton like a devil and into Admiral Street. Benton's a little run-down place. There was a time when the tall chimneys smoked day and night and the people lived and died in the rows of drab houses clus-tered round the mills they worked in. But most of the mills have been closed for years and Benton people now go to work in towns where industry still hums. My dad used to say that Benton couldn't change with the times so it died. It was dead, all right. So was my dad.

I stood and panted, looking along Admiral Street and hating it. I hated everything. I hated the rest of the world and wanted to hurt it.

Admiral Street was deserted except for a cat which walked stiffly into the alley that led to the backs and the bins. Niggers lived in Admiral Street. My mother called them Niggers and worried because so many of them going to Benton School meant that I must mix with them.

'They're different,' she'd sometimes say, trying to explain what she didn't understand. 'It can't be long since they were savages. You can't expect them to know how to behave.' She spoke as one might speak of a horse or a dog, without malice in her voice. There was never any malice in any part of her. 'They aren't like us. One of these days they will be, but it'll take time.'

So she unconsciously dripped acid into my brain until I almost believed her. I searched the Negro boys at school for differences and found none except colour. They were ordinary boys – Hector Robinson, Charlie McArthur, Darkie Bates and the rest – and they fought and footballed as well as most of us and laughed as often. They were part of school, part of life, and I forgot they were different until my mother reminded me.

Many of them lived in Admiral Street, in the oldest part of Benton, built when black-faced white men were piling up the moon-mountain called the Tip and burrowing out fortunes for the few. Admiral Street was old all right, but it was as neat and trim then as any street of terrace houses can be, and it was quieter than most streets. My mother never walked through it. Somehow she was embarrassed by the coloureds who lived in every house.

'They don't understand our ways,' she'd say. 'They

stare so with those dark eyes of theirs and they hang about in the street all day.'

Nobody was staring at me. Nobody was hanging about. This was another of the things my mother was mixed up over, but I'd put things right for her. I'd turn Admiral Street into the din and degradation she thought it ought to be.

There were two jagged stones in the gutter, cat-ammunition spilled from some boy's pocket. I picked them up, fitted my first finger round one and hurled it. It flew straight and spinning and the nearest gaslamp exploded and I yelled. I ran the length of the street and I knew that black noses were flattening against windows and doors were opening. I threw the other stone at the last gaslamp and I missed it, and the stone hit a door and left a white scar on the paint.

I stopped and looked back. A woolly-headed Negro in bright shirt and braces opened the damaged door, stared first at the scar and then at me and looked so worried that I wanted to laugh. The street was filling with people, all of them black, yet there was no din. There wasn't even any dislike. The eyes watching me were gently sad, and to stop myself shrivelling up I yelled.

'You shouldn't ought to do that, boy,' a soft voice rumbled.

I ran again, cutting across the cindery desert where nothing but willowherb and razorgrass had grown for a century. I collected a dozen stones and made for the open end of Gaskin Street, a white-people's street. My mother didn't like Gaskin Street any more than she liked Admiral Street. Mugsy Jones, who'd been in court three times for stealing, lived in Gaskin Street, and old Burnett the watchman at Sadler's, and half a dozen women who went charring at the big houses out Chelford way.

'They're not nice people,' she'd say. 'That Jones boy's a downright hooligan.'

9

But he's got a dad, I thought as I stood at the end of the street. And he's his own dad; not one who's somebody else's; not a secondhand dad.

I took one of the stones out of my pocket. Four girls were playing hopscotch in a pitch chalked on the footpath half-way along the street, and opposite them two aproned women talked across the six feet that separated their front doors. One of them was laughing. She was fat and her folded arms reminded me of skinned lambs in Morris's butcher's shop.

I threw my stone at the nearest gaslamp, twenty yards away. It curved in the air and rattled off a house into the street. The two gossiping women gaped at it as if it were a meteorite.

'Bert!' one of them called.

I threw again and missed. I filled one hand with stones from my pocket and machine-gunned the gaslamp. The last stone hit the glass and scattered it in a glittering spray across the street.

'Bert!' the woman squealed.

The other, the fat one, muttered, 'Little devil!' and stalked towards me like a gorilla, her arms bouncing heavily against her sides. A man peered out of a doorway on the other side of the street; a thin little man who peeled a cigarette off his bottom lip and called, 'What's up, Florrie? What's all the din?'

I shouted and ran. I went back across the cindery desert and on down the slope to the low ground where every spring the frogs spawned in the pools that scummily persisted even through the hot weather. I chased a cat up the slope and climbed the wall at the top of it. I was still yelling rebellion, my voice so ugly that at last I silenced it and sat panting on the wall.

I was looking at Cleworth Street, a ghost street where a cotton mill had died years before. The mill was still standing across the street, its bricks as black as old bones and its tiny windows shattered and blind. Benton people always called it 'Cleworth's', although nobody had worked in it for thirty years and no Cleworth had lived in Benton for half a century.

Dropping off the wall, I walked carefully through the brambles that clutched at my jeans. I picked up half a brick and hurled it at Cleworth's and felt better for the noise of its explosion. I was looking for another when a car nosed round the corner; a small white car which was stopped by the rubble in the road. Its doors swung open and two policemen climbed out of it. One of them pushed his cap off his forehead and stood watching me, his hands on his hips: the other strode through desolation towards me. I saw his big shiny boots flatten the brambles and I was afraid. I wanted to run, but there was no way out except over the wall and back into the vengeance of Gaskin Street.

Then I heard a soft whistle and saw a shadow moving in the darkness inside Cleworth's empty doorway and I ran. I heard the policeman's shout and the thud of the big boots as he leapt after me, but I was through the doorway and in the gloom, and Hector Robinson's rubbery black face was an inch from my nose.

'C'mon, boy!' he whispered.

I followed him, amazed at his supple speed as he flitted over the rubbish on the brick floor. I watched only his back, yet the fringe of my vision registered old wheels and pulleys below the ceiling and strands of the belts which had once brought life to machines long since carted away for scrap.

Hector flew up rickety wooden stairs and, following him, I ran on to a floor that sagged under my weight like an old mattress. Piles of rubbish were cocooned in spiders' webs. I'd never been into this forbidden territory before and I was afraid.

'C'mon, boy!' Hector whispered.

We ran across the floor and through a narrow opening in the wall. We were in a tiny room, a prison cell, with one small window near its ceiling and another boy standing on a crate and looking out.

Without turning his head he said, 'You got him O.K., Robbo?'

'I got him,' Hector said. 'Now hush your noise, Darkie, while we listen.'

The other boy was Darkie Bates and I wondered what my mother would say if she knew I was hiding from the police among Cleworth's cobwebs with two Nigger-boys. For a second my desperate rage came back and I moaned.

'Sh!' Hector whispered.

He was listening. I could see one of his long ears turned to the opening in the wall and I listened with him, and I heard the big shiny boots stealthily crunch on the ground-floor bricks. I crept into a corner and a cobweb net, clinging softly, covered my face. I shuddered and knocked it away. Cobwebs hung everywhere, tapestries of them. Spiders had taken over from Cleworth's dead spinners.

The big boots moved away through the rubbish, paused and moved again, and then Darkie whispered, 'He's off!'

A car door slammed and an engine roared. Darkie went on watching from the little window for a time and then he chuckled and turned round.

'Scuffers has gone, Robbo,' he said, his voice resonating like a drum.

'Then you come down boy,' Robbo said.

Darkie dropped to the floor and Robbo hitched up his jeans and eased his rump on to the crate, his long legs stretched in front of him.

'Now you, Danny Rowley,' he said, 'you tell me what you been up to. The scuffers were after you, boy, and they don't go after kids for nothing – 'specially not white kids. What you been up to?'

I shrugged. These two were my own age and in my form at school and I wasn't afraid of either of them; not even of Robbo who was so tall and slim and smooth.

'We showed you our hiding-place, boy,' he said. 'Me and Darkie's the only ones know this place. Here's where we hide.'

'From the coppers?' I asked.

He looked at me solemnly for a moment. 'You know we ain't had trouble with the scuffers, Danny Rowley. We don't get into that sort of trouble. That right, Darkie?'

Darkie grunted. 'Our dads'd belt us if we did.'

'What our dads'd do,' Robbo said, 'would be a million times worse than any scuffer.'

'Then who do you hide from?' I asked.

The two Negro boys looked at each other and Darkie's face split into a grin.

'We just *hide*, Dan. That's all.'

'Times we come for a smoke,' Robbo said. 'Times we come so's nobody but us know where we are. You ever think what it's like when nobody but you in the whole world knows where you are?'

I shook my head.

'It's kind of excitin', boy,' he said. 'You wanna try it. That's what we kept this place secret for. Now it's spoiled 'cos you know about it and you won't tell us what the scuffers was after you for. O.K. You don't tell us.'

'I'd been smashing gaslamps,' I said.

Robbo sighed. 'Thought maybe you'd been with that Mugsy Jones. But smashin' gaslamps is bad enough. How many did you smash?'

'One in Gaskin Street and one in your street.'

'What did you want to do that for?' Darkie asked.

'I don't know, do I? I just wanted to.'

Darkie stared at me and then grinned. 'To see if you dare? Was that it, Dan? I bet it was.'

'It gives you a nice sort of belly-ache darin' yourself to do something,' Robbo said. 'Trouble is they'll blame us. Anything smashed within a mile of Admiral Street and they blame us.'

'How can they?' I said. 'People saw me do it. It was me the coppers were after, wasn't it?'

Robbo nodded. 'They blame us and I'm going to belt you, boy.'

My anger came back, hot in my face. 'You just try!'

He nodded again. 'They blame us and I'll do more than try.'

'He'll belt you, all right,' Darkie said. 'Robbo can belt anybody when he tries and that's a fact.'

'Bet he can't belt Mugsy Jones,' I said.

'I never tried,' Robbo said. 'Mugsy's older and bigger.'

'I'm the same age and smaller,' I said, 'and you never tried me, and if you do you'll get a shock.'

He gave me a thoughtful look. 'I never wanted to belt you, but if I had to I'd do it. Mugsy too. I'd belt him. If you want to do anything hard enough you can do it.'

'Like you smashin' gaslamps, Dan,' Darkie said. 'You wanted to and you did it. What's your dad going to do to you?'

Robbo shook his head sadly. 'You never was very smart, was you, Darkie? You forgot, boy, that Danny Rowley's got no dad?'

I was almost choking. My chest and throat were aching with resentment and despair and I turned and ran away, down the stairs and out of the mill. I don't remember that I thought about where I was running to. I just ran. I ran right through Benton until I came to our street and saw two cars parked outside our house. One was *his* and the other was the little white police car.

I stood panting for a minute or two and then I hurried

along the street while half a dozen silenced kids watched me. Our house was the seventh in the row of houses, all better than Admiral Street houses because they had tiny front gardens. Ours had a privet bush in the middle of it and nothing else. My dad had always filled it with dahlias and turned it into a bright square of colour, but I couldn't grow dahlias.

I saw one of the coppers sitting in the police car. It was the one with his cap on the back of his head. He watched me as I turned in at our gate.

2 Hooligan

They were all there in our sitting-room; the copper with the big shiny boots, *him* and my mother, looking hot and flustered.

'Danny . . .' she said, and then ran out of words.

The copper had short bristly hair and a red face as shiny as his boots. His cap, with a note-book resting on it, was on his knee.

'Why did you do it, son?' he asked me.

He said nothing. He never did say much when I was around. He was a big man, a bit older than my mother, and I always had the feeling that he was scared of me. He wasn't; he was big and grown-up and had a kid of his own, but that was the feeling I had.

'Do what?' I said to the copper.

He sighed. 'Look, son. Don't try being funny with me or I'll put you in the car and take you to the station where you can be funny with the Inspector. You broke a gaslamp in Gaskin Street and another in Admiral Street. What for?'

''Cos I wanted to,' I said.

Then my mother started. I don't think I'd ever seen her angry before. I'd seen her sad and worried often enough, but I don't think I ever saw her really angry before that night. She walked across the room and swung me round to face her. She bent forward to look at me. There was no need for her to bend because I was nearly as tall as she was, but to her I was still a kid.

'Danny Rowley!' she said in a new, snapping voice. 'I'm not having you disgrace me like this. Next thing you'll be going to court and they'll send you away. What sort of a boy are you? I didn't bring you up to be a hooligan. You answer this policeman properly, my lad. Remember that you're the one who's done wrong. I don't know what your dad would have said.'

The last few words did it. I fought for a second or two, until my throat almost burst, and then I exploded into tears, baby tears. I turned away to hide my shame and I heard *him* say, 'Easy, Edith. Don't be too hard on the lad.'

I swung back on him. 'You keep out of this!' I shouted. 'It isn't anything to do with you!' My mother slapped my face.

I think it was the first time she'd ever hit me, and the stinging pain in my cheek shocked me so much that my tears stopped. Then she started to cry, softly, covering her eyes and moaning, and *he* stood up and put his arm round her shoulders and patted her and made embarrassed, soothing noises. I could have kicked him.

'None of this needed to happen, son,' the copper said. 'All I wanted to know was why you smashed a couple of gaslamps.'

'I was mad,' I said.

He shook his head. 'I get mad sometimes but I don't go round smashing gaslamps.'

My mother blew her nose. 'I told him that Mr Higgins and I are going to be married.'

'Married,' the copper said.

He was still patting her shoulder. 'We're getting married soon,' he said. 'It would be a bit of a shock for the lad.'

The copper stood up, easing his note-boot back into his breast pocket. 'I'll have to put a report in and then it's up to the Chief. He's fed up with young vandals and he may make a case of it. It's up to him.'

'Must you?' my mother asked.

''Fraid so, Mrs Rowley,' the copper said. 'It was reported to the station, you see, and we got the call.'

He made for the door and I said, 'I bet it was the Niggers who snitched.'

His hand, reaching for the door-handle, stopped and he stood still for a moment. Then he slowly turned and looked down at me.

'It was the *Niggers* who hid you in Cleworth's so's I couldn't find you,' he said. 'Young Robinson and Bates. They're always in that place, although I keep telling them it isn't safe. The report about you came from somebody in Gaskin Street. D'you know any *Niggers* in Gaskin Street?'

He watched me for a moment longer, looking at me as he must often have looked at Cleworth's rats when he was on night patrol, and then he turned and opened the door and walked out.

I wanted to die or vanish or be in Australia. I wanted to be anywhere but where I was, in the corner with my shame, and Mother blowing her nose and *him* easing her on to a chair. I turned towards the door and he said, 'Danny', and I stopped. I don't know why I stopped, but I did. I didn't turn to face him. I stood there looking at the door without seeing it and I listened.

'We're going to be married,' he said. 'Your mother and me. You may think we're old but we aren't and we've the right to some life. There'll be you and our Lorna and us – four. We could make a nice family. It's up to you. But remember one thing. You may not like the idea, but you can't stop it.'

He finished and I was released and went upstairs to my room, thinking about him. I sat on my bed, still thinking. Mr Higgins; Walter Higgins; Walter, *Dad*. I sniffed. He was 'Walter' to my mother – from her lips his name sounded like a crime – but he'd never be 'Dad' to me. He lived on the Chelford side of Benton and he had a workshop in an old building in Birley Lane, not far from the colliery. He was an electrician who'd started his own business and now had three men working for him. I'd seen his girl Lorna but I didn't know her well. She went to our school and she was too stuck-up to mix with the kids who lived in Benton's older streets. I knew one or two lads who fancied her, but none of them had ever done more than turn her nose into the air. Joe Carr, my mate, my special friend, thought she was smashing, but I kept away from her. She was a girl, and girls were a secret society with strange rites and signals I didn't understand. I understood football better.

Her mother had been dead for eighteen months. I remembered it because it was one of these things grownups whisper about, sad sympathy in their voices and excitement in their eyes. Lorna Higgins had had a brother, fifteen at the time, who'd drowned in a canoeing accident on the canal, and a fortnight later Mrs Higgins had died suddenly. I remembered that somebody had mentioned gas.

I sat on my bed and I blamed Mrs Higgins. I hated her for being dead. Her death had made it possible for Walter Higgins to marry my mother.

The next morning it was school and Joe Carr came for me. My mother was quiet and tired-looking, but there was a determination in her eyes which was new to me. She hustled me along over breakfast and had my dinner-money out before I could ask for it and she straightened my tie and I was ready and waiting for Joe at the front door. I saw him running along our street. He was a fair-headed lad with freckles that spread in regiments from his nose to his cheeks, and he was always running. He was the best footballer I knew and I was sure that in a few years he'd be playing for a First Division club.

We'd only gone five yards when he said, 'What's up, Dan? What's all this about the coppers last night?'

I growled. 'Somebody's been talking!'

'Somebody! Everybody! Every kid I've seen's told me how a police-car and two coppers came for you last night. You done a murder or something?'

I told him about the gaslamps and Cleworth's and about the policeman who had to make a report to the Chief, and when I'd finished we were half-way to school and he said, 'Flippin' heck!'

We walked for a hundred yards while he thought about it and then he said, 'Hope my mam doesn't stop me going out with you, Dan. She might. My dad wouldn't, but my mam might. She doesn't like me going with kids who've been in court, like Mugsy Jones.'

'I haven't pinched anything!' I said.

He nodded. 'But you're one of them delinquents, aren't you? What *is* a delinquent, Dan?'

'Me!' I said. 'According to you.'

'Why'd you do it, Dan? Was it for fun?'

'Fun!' I said. 'It isn't funny smashing gaslamps. Funny's about the only thing it isn't. It's exciting and daring and frightening and a lot more things, but it isn't funny.'

'Then what did you do it for?'

''Cos I was mad.'

He looked at me and then he nodded. 'I can imagine. You don't often get mad, not like most kids, but when you do you aren't safe. Wouldn't like you to get mad at me. What was it made you mad?'

So I told him about my mother and Walter Higgins and he said, 'Flippin' heck! Fancy livin' in the same house as that Lorna Higgins!'

I growled and he gave me an anxious look and then he said in his stubborn voice, the voice that means he thinks he's right, 'I dunno what you got so mad about. Walter Higgins is O.K. I know Jimmy Taylor who works for him, and Jimmy says he's a decent bloke. If my dad was dead I wouldn't mind havin' Walter Higgins for my dad.'

'Your dad isn't dead!' I growled at him.

'I know; but if he was, I mean.' He looked at me shyly. 'You don't often get mad, Dan, like I said, and don't you get mad at me. If Walter Higgins was your dad you'd always be sure of a job. And fancy havin' Lorna Higgins for your sister!'

He blushed so brightly that I saw it even out of the corner of my eye.

I said, 'You can have her!'

He had gone quiet, thinking, puzzling over some problem.

'Dan,' he said. 'If Walter Higgins was your dad would Lorna be your sister? She wouldn't, would she?'

'Who cares?' I said.

'She'd be your half-sister or step-sister or something, wouldn't she?' He thought for a moment. 'Can you marry your step-sister, Dan? You know, there's some people you can't marry, like your grandmother. Can you marry your step-sister?'

'Belt up!' I snarled at him.

We were joining the crowds converging on the school drifting in noisy battalions towards the old red-brick place that towered above a cluster of prefab classrooms like a hen among chickens. It was a secondary modern school: it was drab and makeshift, yet it was good. It had the best football team for miles around and it had Wally Sinton for its headmaster, and he'd been an international. He was getting on, but now and then he'd come to the playing-field, and you only had to watch him kick a ball to learn more about beauty and power and poetry than you'd learn in a day sitting at a desk, polishing your pants on a hard chair.

I had a look at Lorna Higgins that morning in the hall while we were waiting for Wally Sinton to find a hymn.

She was my age, but she was in a different form. I turned to look at her and caught her staring at me as if she'd never seen me before. She swung away, but not quickly enough to hide the glitter of dislike in her eyes. I knew then that Walter Higgins had told her and I wondered if she guessed how much I hated him.

I could see why so many of the lads fancied her: she was pink and perfect, like a doll, and about as friendly.

That morning at playtime I was in the playground with Joe when Mugsy Jones came up. He was a big fourth-year lad with loose lips and greasy hair. He slouched along, sliding his feet on the ground and never moving quickly except when the coppers were chasing him. He shambled towards us, the little cloud of first-year kids that went everywhere with him, like pilot-fish with a shark, darting round him.

'Hey, kid!' he said. 'You joined the boys?'

I looked straight at him. Most kids were afraid of him but I wasn't. They were afraid of him because he was bulky, like a gorilla, and because he'd been to court. He never had a fight because nobody ever dared to challenge him. He sometimes tortured little kids for sweets or fags or money, but nobody ever fought him. I always had the feeling that one day somebody would fight him and expose the real Mugsy, show up the cowardice hidden inside the bulk. That was why I'd never been afraid of him.

'Which boys?' I asked.

He grinned. 'The coppers' boys! That's who, kid. You had 'em after you last night. You'll be going to court. You want any advice and you come to Mugsy.'

'And what would he have to pay?' somebody said. 'You don't give nothin' away, boy. You want him to fetch you a packet of fags so's you'll tell him how to get sent away for sure?'

It was Robbo, with Darkie Bates trailing him like a

shadow. Robbo was a second-year lad, yet he was as tall as Mugsy but only half as broad. Mugsy glowered at him.

'You'd best clear off, black kid!'

Robbo looked sad. 'I just want to listen, boy. I thought maybe I could use a bit of expert advice for when the scuffers were after me.'

'First time they come after you,' Mugsy said, 'it'll be to put you in a cage and send you back to the jungle.'

One or two of the first-year kids giggled, but Mugsy didn't. I was watching him and I saw the fear in his eyes as he looked at Robbo, and I almost cheered because I knew then that I'd been right about him. Robbo was smiling. At least his lips were smiling, but there were dark and undefinable lights in his eyes.

He said very quietly to Mugsy, 'One of these days, boy, you're gonna say something like that and you're gonna be sorry ever afterwards.'

He walked away, taking Darkie with him, and Mugsy growled, 'Niggers!' and turned back to me.

'Hear your mam's going to get married to that Walter Higgins – him as has the place in Birley Lane.'

'What's it to you?' I said, and then, glaring at Joe, 'Somebody's been blabbing!'

His freckles crowded together in concern. 'Not me, Dan! I never told a soul!'

'I got my spies out, kid,' Mugsy said, 'Isn't much I don't hear about. With Walter Higgins for your dad you'll be worth knowin', Walter's got dough.'

'He'll never be my dad!' I whispered.

Mugsy's eyebrows went up. 'You mean you don't like the idea?'

'I mean I had a dad – a real one.'

Mugsy's cunning little eyes searched mine and then he nodded. 'It's hard cheese, kid. He's goin' to marry your old woman and you can't do a thing about it.'

23

'I'll think of something,' I said.

'So you'd best think fast.'

'Why?'

Mugsy grinned. 'Ain't you heard? The word is that they're gettin' married any day now.'

I didn't believe him. I didn't want to believe him and I wouldn't let myself believe him.

' 'S'right,' he said. 'Tell you what, kid. I'd like to help you. You come round the back of the pit tonight and I'll see what I can do. I'll be in the old shed round about seven. You come and I'll think up a few things Walter Higgins won't like.'

'I'll think up things for myself,' I said, and I jerked my head at Joe and walked away.

The whistle shrilled the end of playtime.

3 Burglar

Tea was ready when I got home that day. Usually we didn't have tea till half past five, which had been my dad's time. It suited my mother better, too, because she worked mornings in Benton Co-op grocery department, serving women who had husbands. But that day tea was ready at half past four, and that wasn't the only surprise. My mother had had her hair fixed. She had soft brown hair and plenty of it, but now it was crimped and pressed into tight waves like the hair of a Greek statue.

I looked at the table and then at her and I said, 'What's going on?'

'Wash your hands, Danny,' she said, 'and come and get your tea.'

She didn't look at me once and I knew there was some guilt in her mind. She gave her hair a useless pat and pushed a plate across the table and I went into the kitchen. I leaned on the sink, thinking and squeezing soap bubbles out of my fists, and suddenly I knew what was going on.

I rushed back to her wet-handed and I shouted, 'You did it! You got married to *him*!'

Her face flamed. I thought at first it was guilt, but instead it was anger.

'You dry your hands, my lad!' she snapped at me, 'and come and get your tea.'

Her voice wasn't loud as mine had been, but there was

25

a stranger's unfriendliness in it. Something had grown between her and me, something ugly and angry that Walter Higgins must have put there.

When we were having tea she said, 'You remember that I don't have to ask your permission if I want to do anything. Remember that I'm your mother and it's been a struggle the last two years.'

Her voice faltered and I studied my plate and couldn't look at her. Before, when she cried, I would put my arm round her and try to console her as a man might, but that was when we both had the same grief.

'I'll get married just when I want to,' she said.

She was calm again, but that ugly anger was still between us, more solid than the table.

We ate in a silence which was a pain to me and then she said, 'I'd have thought you'd have wanted me to have what's best for me. But you're being selfish. You're just thinking of yourself.'

There was a whine in her voice I'd never heard before.

'I'm thinking of my dad,' I muttered.

She didn't hear me. I'd knocked the salt over and she was staring at the little white grains which had fanned across the table.

'Danny!' she said as if I'd done it purposely. 'It's bad luck. Throw some over your left shoulder.'

'I won't!' I said. 'It's daft!'

She leaned forward, pressing her hands on the table until I could see the veins in them like cords. 'Throw some over your shoulder! Do as you're told! We had enough bad luck in the last two years.'

It was so important to her that I was scared. She was quickly changing into somebody I didn't know. I pinched some salt between my finger and thumb and hurled it over my shoulder.

'We're still having bad luck, if you ask me!' I muttered.

'I'm not asking you,' she said.

We'd almost finished tea before she spoke again. She said, 'Tidy yourself up after tea, Danny.'

'Can't I go and see Joe? I don't have to be tidy for him.'

'What about your homework?'

I shook my head. 'Got none. They didn't give us any. It's only old Jacko who gives us homework. Him and his bloomin' maths! So can I go to Joe's?'

She shook her head. 'You're having a visitor.'

I looked at her, trying to catch her eye and hold it. '*Me!* Who?'

'Walter ... Mr Higgins is coming ...'

I snorted. 'He isn't coming to see *me*!'

'He's bringing Lorna with him.'

I couldn't believe it. That stuck-up snooty girl coming to our house.

'She's a nice little girl, Danny,' my mother was saying, but I wasn't listening.

I'd had another thought. I looked at the ceiling with its dark shadows like thunder-clouds over television and fireplace; at the carpet, worn in places so thin that the backing showed through; at the sideboard and table, once good and still shining, but as old as history. And Lorna Higgins was coming here; coming from the big semi she lived in to our old house, a terrace house as dilapidated as the industry that had built it. I could feel shame smouldering inside me.

'Try to be nice to her, Danny,' my mother was saying. 'There's a good boy.'

I wasn't a good boy, but I went upstairs after tea and went to my room and stuck my hair down with spit. I studied myself in the cracked mirror and I saw more clearly than ever how ugly I was. My nose was too big, my ears stuck out; there was a pimple on my chin. I was a mess.

27

They came about seven o'clock. My mother opened the door and they came into our sitting-room and saw me in my chair, barricaded behind a comic. Lorna Higgins was wearing slacks and she looked like a little boy in a soap advertisement. Her father was shy. You don't expect grown-ups to be shy but he was. I watched his embarrassment and grinned savagely into my comic. Lorna was staring round the room, at the bad places I was so ashamed of.

''Lo, Danny!' Walter Higgins said. 'I bet you and Lorna know one another pretty well, don't you?'

I wasn't going to answer him, but my mother didn't give me the chance.

'Danny!' she snapped at me. 'Put that comic down and stand up! Try to be a gentleman for once!'

She'd never told me to be a gentleman before. How can a boy of twelve be a gentleman, anyway? But she'd told me now, and in front of a snooty girl, and I could have killed her' and Walter Higgins and Lorna Higgins and myself.

I stood up, groaning, and Lorna Higgins slowly swung her eyes, big and glittery and blue, on to me and looked at me as if I had two heads. I stood it for as long as I could and then I said, 'Seen enough?'

That jolted her. She flushed and my mother gave a little moan.

Walter Higgins chuckled. 'Good for you, Danny. She shouldn't stare and she's always doing it.'

'She was doing it this morning in school,' I said. 'Staring at me as if I was something in a zoo.'

Lorna flushed again. 'I was not! You're a . . .'

She ran out of words and my mother said, 'Well, let's sit down.'

My mother and Walter Higgins sat one on each side of the fireplace, Walter Higgins in my dad's chair which was now mine. That left me to sit on the settee with

Lorna but, although it was only a small settee, I managed to squeeze away from her.

'Had a good day, Walter?' my mother asked.

He nodded. 'Been out at Thorley. Doing the wiring for all the new houses Sadler's are building. Lot of work there. Sub-contract stuff.'

Lorna Higgins said to me, 'Got a record-player?'

I shook my head without looking at her and my mother said, 'It's nice at Thorley. I used to have an aunt lived there when it was all country.'

'It's still country,' Walter Higgins said. 'I don't know if it will be when Sadler's have finished. Nice residential development, they're doing.'

'Got a transistor?' Lorna asked me in a purring-cat voice.

'No!' I said. 'And I don't want one.'

'It'll be a grand estate when it's finished,' Walter Higgins was telling my mother. 'About a couple of hundred houses and bungalows – good-class ones.'

'But where are all the people coming from?' my mother asked. 'Benton isn't a big place and it isn't growing.'

They were talking only to fill the silence. They might just as well have been talking about the weather.

'Got a car?' Lorna whispered.

There was plenty of purpose in what she was saying. I ignored her.

'Over-spill,' Walter Higgins said. 'Grimthorpe's growing fast and Thorley'll take some of the over-spill.'

'What *have* you got?' Lorna asked me, and I snarled at her, '*A mother!*'

I saw both their faces jerk round to me, my mother's twisted with pain and Walter Higgins's startled, and then I was rushing out of our back door, across the yard and through the gate. I kept on rushing, without a thought for where I was going, and suddenly I was turning into Cleworth Street and stumbling across its rubble.

I leaned, panting, against the old mill, and Robbo said, 'The scuffers after you again, boy?'

He was there, inside the doorway, doubly dark in the last of the day's light. I could see only his eyes and his shining teeth until he stepped out, scowling at me.

'You in bad trouble again, Dan Rowley?' he asked me.

'Trouble!' I said. 'Not copper trouble. Home trouble. My mother'll kill me and I don't care if she does.'

He nodded thoughtfully. 'Home trouble's bad. Ain't nothing worse than home trouble. What you gonna do?'

He wasn't like other kids; wasn't like any kid I knew. He didn't try to pry into my troubles or offer me useless sympathy.

I shook my head and he said, 'You scared to go home?'

I didn't say anything. I didn't know. I was scared more of the deep rebellious mutterings inside me than of my mother's anger.

'You come to our house if you want,' he said, suddenly shy. 'I got a big bed and my mamma'd let you sleep with me. You do that if you want.'

I could feel the tears fighting their way to the surface. With me it was always like that. Anger or tragedy would leave me dry-eyed and screwed-up inside, but kindness would make the tears spout.

I stared at him and he said, 'You seen Mugsy Jones tonight, like he told you?'

Mugsy came into my mind, a release from kindness, and turned off my tears.

'No,' I said, 'but it's an idea.'

'A bad one. That Mugsy's no good. My dad ...'

'Your dad's like everybody else!' I snarled at him.

Everybody's against Mugsy and they never give him a chance. It isn't fair! Some people never get a proper chance!'

I left him staring and I ran, taking all the short-cuts I knew but avoiding our street. I turned into Birley Lane, and at the bottom of it I came to the open ground and the twisted iron railings round the forbidden property of the old mine. The pit-head gear towered into the sky, topped by the black circles of the rusted wheels that hadn't turned for ten years.

There were gaps in the railings and I squeezed through the first and made for the shed. Grass struggled in the cindery crust of coal-dust deposited years before. The shed was open and I craned forward to look into its gloom. Mugsy wasn't there. There was an empty wooden box and an old brew-can on its side in one corner, and a loop of tarry string over a nail in the wall, but there was no sign of Mugsy.

It was almost dark and suddenly I was afraid. There was about the old colliery that strange, knowing silence that comes to places after men have done with them.

I turned and dashed back through the fence and into Birley Lane, and I didn't stop until I could hear sounds again, the subdued throb of Benton and the rumble of traffic on the distant motorway.

Birley Lane was deserted. Only cats and courting couples used it at night, liking its quietness. Nobody had lived in it for years and most of its buildings were dere-lict and empty. Just a few of them were still used as warehouses and workshops.

I hurried along, thinking that I should go home and face them, and I came to Walter Higgins's place and stopped, puzzled, in front of its doors. They were big and green and double, and his name was painted in white across them, 'WALTER' and 'H' on one and 'IGGINS' on the other. In the door on the left there was another smaller door, and it was this that had puzzled me. It was open.

It wasn't wide open but it wasn't closed and locked, and I wondered why, because Walter Higgins was a careful man. I pushed it with the tips of my fingers and, as it swung back, I heard a noise like the scurry of rats across a floor. I thought that the best thing would be to go home and tell him and perhaps deflect my mother's anger. Then I thought that I didn't care if his workshop was full of rats and if all its doors were open.

I stepped quietly through the open door. It was dark inside and so silent that I could hear the quick beat of my heart and another beat, like the echo of mine. Some light still came in through the windows high in the walls and I could see a switch close to me, beside the door. I reached out and pressed it and nothing happened for a second. Then there were a few sputtering flashes and the sudden white light of fluorescent tubes.

Somebody whispered, 'Put the perishin' light out, kid!'

I stared round the workshop, my eyes searching. I could see the little office behind a glass partition at the far end and the benches covered with electricians' junk and the wooden racks on the wall filled with conduit tubing, and behind them Mugsy Jones blinking at me, his mouth forming curses.

'What are you doing?' I said.

He came in a rush and behind him came another lad. I turned to dive through the doorway, but one of them grabbed me and the lights were knocked off.

'I got 'im, Mugsy!' the other lad shouted.

I knew him. He was Snotty Smith, a toothy, thin-faced lad whose nose was always twitching like a rabbit's. He was in Mugsy's class at school. I drove my elbow into his stomach and he wheezed but held on to me.

Mugsy said, 'Take it easy, kid. We ain't gonna hand you to the coppers.'

'Coppers! *Me!*'

I could just see his grin. 'We was helpin' you, kid. We waited for you but you didn't come so we got started.'

'Helping me? How d'you mean?'

'What we was talkin' about in school today. You not likin' havin' Walter Higgins for your old man. You wantin' to get your own back on him.'

Then I understood. 'You mean you thought I'd help you break into his workshop? You're daft! I may not like Walter Higgins, but I'm not going to court and being sent away just to prove it. You broke in here – you and Snotty – and it's you two who'll go to court and get sent away.'

A smile twisted Mugsy's face. 'This kid's got a hole in his head, Snotty. You heard him. Trying to put the blame on us.'

'Charming!' Snotty said. 'After all we done for him.'

'His new dad isn't going to like it,' Mugsy said.

'He isn't my dad!' I shouted.

'Quiet, kid,' Mugsy said. 'You'll have the coppers here and they won't like it when we tell 'em how me and Snotty watched you fiddle with the lock and then go in. That right, Snotty?'

Snotty giggled. 'Right! We watched him all the time.'

'You're a liar,' I said, and he twisted my arm.

'They'll give us a medal or something,' Mugsy said. 'When we tell 'em how we followed you and caught you in the act they'll probably give us a reward. Breaking and entering, that's what they call it, kid, and they send you away for it. This on top of the gaslamp lark'll get you a free ticket to Borstal.'

I could hear his words and I knew that every one of them was a lie, yet I felt certain that they would sound true to the police.

He was laughing at me. 'But don't you worry, kid. We don't hand our mates over to the coppers for any reward. I tell you what. You bring me a dollar to-morrow and we won't say a word. That right, Snotty?'

'How about if we make it ten bob?' Snotty said.

I snorted, 'You're getting nothing out of me!' and I jerked my arm out of Snotty's hand.

'Suit yourself, kid,' Mugsy said. 'It's your funeral, and there's been enough funerals in your family. The coppers don't like thieves, specially them what pinch from their own dads.'

'He isn't my dad!' I fumed. 'And I haven't pinched *anything*!'

'No?' He patted my jacket. 'What you got there, then?'

I plunged my hand into my pocket and stopped when my fingers felt the chill of metal. Slowly I drew out a pair of pliers.

'See what I mean?' Mugsy said. 'Your finger-prints'll be all over them. What the coppers call an open-and-shut case.'

I was staring at the pliers. 'You put them there! You or Snotty Smith!'

'Us?' Mugsy said, all innocence, and I hurled the pliers at him.

He ducked and they hit the wooden doors with the thud of doom and I sprang after them and hit Mugsy flush on his thick lips. He staggered back and Snotty wrapped himself like an octopus round me, and Mugsy lurched at me, his fist drawn back. I yelled my fury and he stopped.

'*Shurrup!*' he hissed. 'You want the coppers to come?'

'Let them come!' I roared. 'I haven't done anything!'

Mugsy peered into my red and roaring face and said, 'He's havin' a fit or something.'

'He's a nut-case,' Snotty said, and he was scared.

'*Police!*' I yelled, and Mugsy darted out of the door. Snotty followed him and I could hear the rush of their feet as they ran away.

I was trembling, but not from fear. When I had one of my kid rages it always left me so weak that I trembled. I switched on the light again to look for the pliers, but there was a mistiness in front of my eyes and I couldn't see them. Mugsy and Snotty were now far away and the only sound was the hiss of one of the lamps. I stepped out of the doorway into the near-darkness outside and I walked slowly along Birley Lane. The street lights were on and in Cronton Road there were youth-packs round bright shop-windows, yelping and smoking.

I walked home and went in the back way, and when I opened the sitting-room door they were still there, just as I'd left them; my mother worried, Walter Higgins stern and Lorna only a tremble from tears.

'Go on, my girl,' he said to her. 'Get on with it.'

She stood up, facing me but not looking at me, and she said in a tight little voice, 'I'm sorry I was rude.'

She spoke quickly, her voice like a plucked guitar string, and she sat down. The things grown-ups do to kids, trying to turn them into copies of themselves! I didn't like Lorna, but I was so sorry for her that I hated Walter Higgins more than ever for making her apologise.

I snorted. 'Who says you were rude? You weren't.'

'She was,' Walter Higgins said in his slow way, talking like a steam-hammer. 'If she's rude she apologises.'

'What she did was nothing to what some people have done,' I told him.

My mother gave a little gasp. 'Now *you* can apologise, Danny,' she said.

I groaned. 'All grown-ups ever want is apologies! What's the use of apologies? Anybody can say he's sorry if he isn't dumb!'

She stood up, her eyes savage, and Walter Higgins said, 'Easy, Edith. He's got something on his mind. What is it, lad?'

I wanted to jolt him and I did. 'I just came along

35

Birley Lane. The door of your place is wide open – that little door. You want to keep it closed and locked at night. There's some bad kids round here – kids who pinch things and smash gaslamps.'

I dared not tell him more because I was afraid that Mugsy's story would sound better than mine. Mugsy had Snotty Smith to bleat confirmation of everything he said, and there were those pliers with my finger-prints all over them.

But I had jolted Walter Higgins. He was on his feet and my mother was taking him and Lorna to the door, and I was laughing like mad to myself.

4 Police

My mother was quiet over breakfast the next morning, quiet and so occupied with her thoughts that she scarcely noticed me. Even when I crunched my corn-flakes viciously, with my mouth open, she didn't notice. She was so thoughtful that she started me thinking; thinking about how I'd been a devil for two days.

I thought about my dad. I remembered the last time I'd seen him in hospital, lying on his back in a bed, his face blue against the antiseptic whiteness of the pillow.

'Be a good lad, Danny,' he'd whispered. 'Do as your mother tells you.'

I'd nodded and left him and the next morning my Aunt Nellie had told me that he was dead. She hadn't used the word 'dead': she'd said 'gone to rest'. Nobody had said 'dead' in our house for months afterwards. 'Passed over' and 'released' and a lot more fancy expressions had been used often enough, but I'd known that they all meant 'dead' and I knew what dead was. It was like when I was a kid and my dog was run over and wasn't a dog any more.

'Do as your mother tells you,' he'd said and I'd nodded. Now she was quiet and she was probably thinking about all the things she'd told me to do and I hadn't done.

Then Joe Carr knocked on our door and I was glad.

I jumped up, chewing toast, grabbed my bag and, escaping from my mother's quietness, I shouted, 'T'ra!'

and dashed out of the house. Joe was there, his football boots slung over his shoulder, and I remembered that we had games in the afternoon, but I wasn't going to face my mother's quietness again for football boots. I'd rather face Sprog's sarcasm or the slipper he sometimes belted you with. He could be so sarcastic that it curled you up, and with that old slipper he could leave a red mark on your backside for hours. He took us for P.T. and he was a good footballer. He'd never been an international or a First Division player, but he was big and he often went through a team of boys like a bear through dogs.

'Heard anything from the coppers?' Joe asked me. I shook my head and he went on, 'Should think you'll be O.K. then. If they'd been going to take you in they'd have sent the Black Maria for you by now.'

'The Black Maria!' I snorted. 'Don't talk daft! That's for criminals – gangsters – not kids.'

'My mam says it's all right for you to go on being my mate,' Joe said. 'I thought I'd better tell her because she'd get to know anyway. She said that any lad who's had as much trouble as you've had can smash as many gas-lamps as he likes, for her. That's what she said.'

'She did, did she?' I was angry and I didn't know why. 'And what's all this trouble I'm supposed to have been in?'

'You know, Dan. Your dad, and...' He blushed, obliterating his freckles. 'You know how your mam's getting married? That's what my mam was on about.'

'She was, was she? Stickin' her nose in! My mother can get married if she wants, can't she? She doesn't have to get your mother's permission, does she?'

I think that Joe and I might have had our only quarrel then, but he'd stopped listening. We were almost at school and he was staring straight in front, his blush now climbing into his scalp and shining through his fair hair. He was staring at Lorna Higgins, standing at the school gate and watching us. When we were close she started to walk towards us.

'It's that . . . that Lorna Higgins!' he muttered.

I grunted. I wondered how a tough, compact lad like Joe who, on the football-field never recognised fear, could be reduced by a girl to stuttering and blushing.

'I can see, can't I?' I growled.

She stopped in front of us, vividly excited. 'My dad's place *was* burgled, Dan! Good thing you spotted that door. The police were there last night and they were going again this morning to look for finger-prints!'

'Finger-prints,' I mumbled, and my hand remembered the coldness of the pliers.

'I'll tell you all about it after dinner,' she said. 'I can't now because we'll be late. You be on the railway bank after dinner and I'll tell you.'

'If you're lucky,' I said, but she had turned and was hurrying towards the gate, her legs like two long pink spindles.

'What's all this, Dan?' Joe asked. 'I'll come with you after dinner.'

I'd forgotten him. I was still thinking about the coldness of the pliers and the finger-prints which had been on them all night.

Nothing much happened that morning except that at playtime Mugsy Jones and Snotty Smith came looking for me. They must have been keen to find me because they'd given up the chance of a playtime smoke in the W.C.s.

Mugsy looked at me, anxious and arrogant at the same time.

'Brought that dollar, kid?' he asked.

He had a bruise on his lip and the sight of it made me savagely glad.

'Somebody give you a thump last night, Mugsy?' I asked him.

39

'Don't push your luck,' he growled. 'I've kept me mouth shut . . . so far.'

Snotty giggled. 'And we won't snitch if you play it right.'

'You never snitch, boy,' Robbo said, his voice rumbling in his chest. He and Darkie Bates had followed Mugsy towards Joe and me. 'You just cadge fags.'

Mugsy's chest jutted out and he took a step towards Robbo, but he stopped, puzzled by the look in Robbo's eyes.

'You thinkin' of tryin' something, Mugsy?' Robbo asked.

'You do and we'll murder you,' Darkie said.

'There's four of us,' Joe said. 'And you've only got Snotty and he couldn't fight a dead cat.'

Snotty squeaked, but nobody took any notice of him. Nobody ever took any notice of Snotty.

'And you best leave Dan Rowley alone,' Robbo said to Mugsy. 'I want to see that boy about some broken glass.'

'You lot better watch out!' Mugsy growled and shambled away.

'What's all this about broken glass?' I said to Robbo.

'First you tell us what's all this about Snotty snitchin'?' he said.

I told them. The secret was bursting to be shared and there were so many people I couldn't tell. I told them about Walter Higgins's place and the pliers and how I'd punched Mugsy in the mouth.

'What you want to do is tell your mamma,' Darkie Bates said, his eyes round and serious.

'Don't be a nit!' I said. 'You know what mothers are like. They're so flippin' honest. She'd go and tell the coppers, and how would I look when Mugsy and Snotty Smith told their story?'

'Bet they've rehearsed it,' Joe said.

Darkie nodded. 'It'd be two on to one.'

Robbo was watching me, his eyes thoughtful. 'You best keep this to yourself, boy. You shouldn't even ought to have told us.' He glanced at Darkie and Joe. 'No talking. You remember.'

They both nodded and Darkie said, 'We could make it four on to two. We could say we were with Dan last night and we saw Mugsy and Snotty break into Walter Higgins's.'

'But we weren't,' Robbo said, 'and we didn't. That's tellin' lies, boy, and kids who tell lies don't go to Heaven.'

'Tellin' lies about the truth, though,' Darkie said. 'I bet that wouldn't stop you going to Heaven.'

Robbo shook his head. 'You tell lies and the scuffers'll catch you out for sure. You tell the truth or you keep your mouth shut. We keep our mouths shut.'

After dinner Joe and I went to the playing-field and across it to the railway embankment that runs along one side of it. There haven't been any trains on that embankment for years, nor even any railway lines for as long as I can remember. It was the line used to haul coal from the colliery and it died when the colliery died. They took the lines away because they were metal and useful to somebody, but who wants an embankment? Only the weeds ever used it once the railway had done with it. They were bursting out of its sides in a spring riot.

Joe and I sat half-way up the slope and we hadn't been there long before Lorna Higgins came hurrying after us, and Joe's blush started to climb up his neck. There was another girl with Lorna, Jessie Watts, a quiet and nervous girl nobody ever noticed.

Lorna started talking while she was still at the bottom of the embankment.

'There wasn't half a mess in my dad's place last night, Dan. He telephoned for the police and they came; two of

41

them and then two more in ordinary clothes. They looked into everything.'

She sat near to me. Jessie Watts had stayed at the bottom of the embankment. I didn't see her look up at us once.

'The burglar'd broken into my dad's office,' Lorna went on, 'and you never saw such a mess! Papers all over the place! He stole about five pounds that my dad keeps in a drawer.'

'Five pounds!' I said, concerned with the cunning of thieves.

She sniffed. 'What's five pounds? It's nothing to my dad. And anyway it's insured.'

'Anything else?' I asked.

'Anything else what?'

I shrugged. 'Did they ... did he pinch anything else? You know ... stuff, tools, and so on.'

'My dad didn't have time to check everything, but he didn't think so. There was a pair of pliers in one corner, where he must have thrown them away when he'd finished with them.'

My heart had stopped.

'The police took them for finger-prints,' she went on. 'They think he used them to open the drawer where the petty cash was.'

'Petty cash?' Joe said. 'What's petty cash, Dan?'

I didn't know but Lorna did.

'What you buy stamps and odds and ends with,' she said, talking to Joe as if he were a little kid from the junior school. Then she gave him a long cold look and said, 'This isn't any of your business. It's private.'

I could have hit her. I was watching Joe's face and I saw his spirit crumple, and I wanted to hurt her as cruelly as she had hurt him.

'If it isn't Joe's business it isn't mine,' I said to her. 'Joe and me's mates and we don't have secrets. You come butting in where you aren't wanted and then you as good as tell Joe to clear off. You're as bad as your dad; butting in and breaking people up.'

For a second or two she didn't move and then, when she turned her head, her face startled me. It was white with two bright spots burning in her cheeks. Her eyes were so fiercely hot that I couldn't look into them.

'*My dad!*' she said in a tremble. 'It's your mother who's butting in where she isn't wanted! Everybody knows how she's been throwing herself at my dad.'

She jumped up and raced down the slope while I was still listening to her words, hearing them over and over in my head and finding it hard to believe that she'd said them. I watched her and Jessie Watts running across the playing-field and I could still hear her words.

'Fierce, isn't she?' Joe muttered. 'Bet any lad who takes her out is sorry for it afterwards. You wouldn't get me to go out with her.'

In the afternoon I began to worry about what Sprog would do when I told him I'd forgotten my games kit. I worried about this until shortly before the lesson, and then Wally Sinton sent for me and I started worrying about something else.

Wally Sinton's room was upstairs and from its window he could see across the playing-field. We often knew that he was watching us, but we didn't mind. He was one of those grown-ups who watch you not to see what you're doing wrong but to see what you're doing right.

That afternoon he was in his room with a man, a big man who managed to look uncomfortable in Wally's easy-chair. They were talking when I went in but they stopped and the man looked at me and I didn't like him. He stared and I never liked people who stared.

'Detective Sergeant Garside, Danny,' Wally Sinton said. 'He's come to ask you about last night. It was you

43

who told Mr Higgins that his workshop had been broken into, wasn't it?'

'I told him the door was open,' I said.

The detective didn't say anything. He sat there in a hunched-up way and he stared at me until I felt as uncomfortable as he looked. I could feel anger hurting my chest and I was ready to ask him if he'd seen enough when Wally Sinton said, 'Right, Sergeant, what do you want to say to him?'

'He's a gaslamp-smasher,' the sergeant said quietly.

Wally Sinton's eyes closed a little and we who knew him, knew what that meant. The sergeant didn't know him.

'So you told me,' Wally Sinton said. 'You told me, too, that he isn't going to be charged, so shall we concentrate on last night's burglary?'

So the lousy copper had snitched to Wally Sinton! I hated him. He was speaking to me, but rage was pounding so furiously in my ears that for a time I didn't hear him. He stopped and stared at me again.

'Well, son?' he said. 'I asked you, are you going to help me.'

'No!' I said.

I spoke quietly enough, just one short word, but it staggered him. To him all kids were criminals who were afraid of him.

Wally Sinton sighed and said, 'Just wait outside the door for a minute, Danny, will you?'

On the other side of the green-painted door I stood and listened to Wally Sinton's voice and felt the quiet force of it. I could see the library at the other end of the corridor and through its glass doors half a dozen Fourth Year kids reading. Wally Sinton often strolled into the library. Two things he liked: football and books. You had only to watch his hands as he opened a good book to know how he felt. They were like the hands of a priest holding a cross; gentle and reverent yet strong with expectation. Then I heard him call to me and I went inside again.

'Just answer the sergeant's questions, Danny,' he said.

I don't know what he'd told that copper while I'd been waiting outside, but he'd changed him and reduced him. The copper looked at me, not at my eyes but at my chest, and a smile twisted his face.

'We got off on the wrong foot, son,' he said. 'When you spend your time with villains you get to thinking everybody's a villain. Now you know that there was a break-in at Higgins's last night, don't you?' I nodded and his eyes flicked suddenly up to my face. 'What do you know about it?'

'They pinched five quid,' I said.

'Who did?'

My mouth opened but nothing came. He'd almost caught me and I knew that although he was a copper, he was a thief for cunning.

'The burglars,' I said. 'Who else?'

'I told you to answer the questions, Danny,' Wally Sinton said. 'I didn't tell you to ask any of your own.'

The copper was looking down at his big spade fingers.

'How did you know?' he asked.

'Lorna Higgins told me.'

'Did she say "burglars"?'

'She must have done because that's what they were, weren't they?'

He smiled. 'They were, son. Except that we don't know they were "they". We don't know if there was one of them or two or three. We've got some ideas, but we don't know. Do you?'

'Do I what?'

'Know how many there were.'

I wondered what he knew, what secrets he was keeping in that big balding head. He didn't ask questions: he set traps. I looked at Wally Sinton and I said, 'Can I ask him a question now, sir?'

'I should think so,' he said.

I looked straight at the copper. 'Why are you asking me all this?'

He nodded. 'A good question, son. I don't have to answer it but I will. You're the only person we know who has any connection with that break-in.'

'How am I connected with it?'

'You reported it.'

I shook my head. 'I didn't. I told Walter Higgins his door was open. That's all I did. I only told him because he was at our house and I knew it would get rid of him and it did.'

He stared at me again and then he said, 'O.K. You told him the door was open. How much was it open?'

'Only a bit.' I spread my finger and thumb a couple of inches apart. 'About that much.'

'Could you see inside?'

'It was too dark.'

'Sure?'

' 'Course I'm sure. It was very nearly dark outside.'

He nodded and then said slowly, 'The lights were on when Mr Higgins got there.'

My heart jerked in my chest. I'd switched the lights on and I must have left them on. The copper had tricked me after all but I'd given nothing away that mattered. He was standing up heavily, like a bull rising from grass.

'Thanks, Headmaster,' he said.

Wally Sinton was looking at me and I looked back at him and knew that the strength I'd felt throughout the whole interview had come from him.

'I hope you felt better after you'd broken those gas-lamps,' he said.

46

I didn't feel better then. My spirit had curled up inside me, but he didn't keep me there to die agonisingly of shame.

'Off you go,' he said, and I went.

5 Fight

There was a football meeting that day at four o'clock and Joe and I were there. We were the only Second Year kids on the first team. Sprog talked to us about tactics and Wally Sinton came in quietly and stood at the back to make sure that Sprog's tactics were right. It was the big match the following Saturday, the last match of the season, and Wally wanted us to win.

'Remember,' he sometimes said, 'you play football to win. Two things you remember: you play football and you win. Both are important, but playing to win is important. If you play any other way it's an insult to your opponent.'

We knew what he meant when he said, 'I'll be there on Saturday.' We knew he'd be on the touchline, never making a sound, but watching us and somehow breathing his determination into us.

After the meeting Joe and I walked home the long way, not plunging straight through Benton but wandering round its tattered edge, and when we reached the top of our street Hector Robinson was waiting for us with Darkie Bates and Charlie McArthur. Charlie was another of the Negro boys from Admiral Street. He was quiet and his eyes were big and round as if he found life a perpetual surprise.

Robbo nodded at me and said, 'We've been waiting a long time, boy. I wanted to see you about some broken glass. You smashed a gaslamp in our street.'

'So what?' I said.

'So you come and you clean up the mess.'

Darkie nodded. 'Our street's always clean, ain't it, Robbo? If it isn't clean people talk. We ain't lettin' you white kids mess it up so's people'll say we're dirty folks.'

'Get lost!' I said.

Charlie McArthur gave me a white-eyed look and said, 'You'd best come, kid, and do like Robbo tells you.'

'And what'll Robbo do if I don't?' I said.

I wanted my tea and these three darkie boys were keeping me waiting.

'I'll belt you,' Robbo said. 'Don't like scrapping. If we're in a scrap with white kids people say it's our fault. Back to the jungle, you black kids! But you don't clean up that mess and I'm gonna belt you.'

'You and who else?' I asked.

'Just me, boy,' Robbo said.

Joe groaned. 'Aw, come on, Dan! I'll help you clean it up.'

'What!' I said. 'Me go street-cleaning for Niggers!'

Robbo hit me. He didn't hit me hard, but his knuckles stung my jaw bone and I staggered back. I stared at him, hating him, and then I flew at him, punching with both hands. Briefly I saw Charlie turn towards me and Joe dive at him in a rugby tackle, and then I saw nothing but Robbo's swaying head and my fists whistling past it and never hitting it. He was smiling and he hit me again, lightly, as if hitting me were easy, and I went mad. I charged him and flung my fists like flails and I didn't touch him once. I might as well have tried to hit the breeze or a shadow, yet suddenly he jerked sideways and almost fell and I stopped, wondering how I had done it.

Then I saw Mugsy Jones grinning at me and gently rubbing the knuckles of his right hand.

49

'You fightin' Niggers, kid?' he said. 'Looked like you were needin' a bit of help.'

Joe was lying on the footpath with Charlie McArthur wrapped round him. Snotty Smith had his fingers entwined in Darkie's thick hair and was pulling his head back. I could have killed Mugsy.

'I didn't need any help from you!' I snarled at him.

Then Robbo glided up to him and hit him with a punch so fast that I never saw it. It caught Mugsy on the jaw and dumped him in the road. Snotty squeaked, released Darkie's hair and backed away, frightened in an instant.

Mugsy was sitting in the road rubbing his jaw and I wished that every kid in school could see him.

'You called me "Nigger", boy,' Robbo said quietly to him. 'You call me "Nigger" again and I'll belt you proper.'

Mugsy scrambled to his feet, keeping warily away from Robbo, and his eyes were vicious.

'Hit me when I wasn't lookin'!' he muttered.

'Don't talk wet!' I said. 'He was right in front of you.'

Mugsy took no notice of me. His hands, hanging low at his sides, were opening and closing slowly while he watched Robbo.

Joe was helping Charlie to his feet. 'You try anything, Mugsy,' he called, 'and we'll murder you! You can't count Snotty and there's five of us.'

'Don't need five,' Robbo said. 'Me and Dan Rowley could massacre them.'

'I'll get the lot of you!' Mugsy rumbled. 'I'll get you one at a time and I'll kick your faces in!'

'You try that and I'll boot you all the way to the police-station,' Walter Higgins said.

He'd come walking silently round the corner and I'd never realised how big he was until I saw him towering over Mugsy. Mugsy didn't argue. He turned and slouched away, his shoulders thrust forward and his head down. Snotty trotted after him.

'You don't forget that gaslamp boy,' Robbo said to me.

'What gaslamp's this?' Walter Higgins asked.

'It's between Robbo and me,' I growled at him, and he shrugged and said, 'O.K. it's between Robbo and you.'

We split up. there, going our different ways. Joe's shyness suddenly overcame him and he raced away at that speed no other kid could keep up with. The three Negro boys slipped round the corner and that left me to walk with Walter Higgins. I couldn't think of anything I wanted to say, but after a minute he said, 'The police been to see you today?'

I nodded and gave him a grunt.

'I didn't want them to,' he said, 'but you're the only one who can help them.'

I grunted again. 'You ought to have heard that copper! You'd have thought it was *me* who'd broken into your place! Anyway, Wally Sinton sorted him out.'

'Sounds like that bald-headed detective,' he said. 'I told him to watch his step. About as tactful as a rhinoceros. I don't suppose he can help it. But you've nothing to worry about. Nobody thinks you had anything to do with it.'

I shivered when I thought of what would happen if Mugsy told his cunning tale and Snotty squealed confirmation.

Walter Higgins had tea at our house that night, and as soon as I'd finished I wanted to go out. I hated being there with them, watching her look at him and him look at her, both of them smiling little smiles that shut me out.

I stood up and said, 'All right if I go?'

'Where are you going?' my mother asked.

I couldn't tell her the truth so I told her a lie. Mothers

turn kids into liars when they try to force all their secrets out of them.

'Joe's,' I said.

She glanced at Walter Higgins. 'It'll be all right, won't it?'

I was so sorry for him that I didn't lose my temper. He was startled and embarrassed and there was some anger in his voice when he answered her.

'It's nothing to do with me! It's up to you, Edith.'

'I just wondered what you thought,' she said.

Then I lost my temper. 'Make your mind up!' I growled at her.

'You see?' she said to him. 'He's getting more difficult every day. Cheeky, too.'

'Look,' he said to her quietly. 'He didn't ask you, could he go and rob a bank. All he wants is to go and play with his pal and he's waiting for you to tell him. Some lads wouldn't even have asked.'

She nodded at me and said, 'Home before dark, Danny. And mind who you play with. And...'

But I was running into the kitchen and out of the house. That was my mother's trouble. She was always giving me advice, and it was the same advice every time so that when she started I knew what was coming next. If Walter Higgins could stop her giving me advice there'd be one good thing would come out of their marriage. But only one. The rest was all bad and nasty and – I thought of my dad for a moment – and a betrayal.

I didn't go to Joe's. I knew that his mother was taking him to see his auntie's new baby that night and that he was fed up because babies embarrassed him. I went instead the other way, to Admiral Street, and I picked up the broken glass that somebody had swept into a neat pile in the gutter.

Admiral Street was as quiet as ever. The deep-throated

laugh of a man in one house made me think of the Congo rolling through jungles as deep as oceans. Then a door opened and a young man, as colourful as a fighting-cock, stood in the doorway watching me and saying nothing.

I carried the broken glass, gingerly held in both hands, to the cindery desert at the end of the street and dumped it there. I didn't want to go back along the street, past the young man and the empty staring windows, so I cut across the desolation and went towards the wall along Cleworth Street. It was late evening and the hollows had filled with shadows. I heard somebody running and I turned round. Robbo and Darkie Bates and Charlie McArthur were chasing after me, Darkie giving me a bright grin.

'You done it, Dan!' he said.

'What?'

'You cleared up that mess of broken glass like Robbo wanted,' he said.

I was about to grunt, but then I noticed that there were people in Admiral Street, black people talking and smiling. I could see Darkie's mother, a squat woman in bulging pinafore, and Robbo's father, almost as tall as the gaslamp.

'It was nice, boy,' Robbo said. 'Nice and friendly.'

'How about if we go to Cleworth's?' Darkie said. 'To our secret place ... all of us.'

Robbo shook his head slowly. 'Them kids would see us.'

He was looking at the end of Gaskin Street, where Mugsy Jones, Snotty Smith and another Gaskin Streeter, Wilf Brady, a second-year kid at school, were leaning against a wall and watching us.

'Don't want no trouble with Mugsy,' Charlie whispered, and he was afraid.

Robbo patted his shoulder. 'Won't be no trouble, boy.'

6 Fury

My mother and Walter Higgins got married the next day and she didn't say a word to me about it.

She was quiet at breakfast. She'd kept her curlers in and her head was clamped in tight ringlets. Her hair was soft and thick and she always brushed it at night and combed it before breakfast.

'What's the idea?' I said to her. 'Your hair looks a mess.'

'I didn't have time,' she said, looking at me across the cup she was holding in front of her mouth. 'We're late. So get on with your breakfast.'

We weren't late but I didn't argue. She was on the other side of the table yet she might have been in another world. When I was ready to go to school she said, 'Just remember, Danny, I've got to do what I think's best for both of us; for me as well as you.'

I puzzled over this until Joe came and then I forgot about it. Joe was talking about Saturday's match against Cronton. Cronton School was three times as big as ours and it had a playing-field like a prairie. We played their first team at the end of every season and it was supposed to be a friendly, but there was nothing friendly about Wally Sinton. I never understood why he was so keen for us to beat Cronton unless it was because Cronton's headmaster came every year to the match and looked at our old school as if it were a historic monument.

Nothing much happened that morning. We had Maths

and English and History, but nothing ever happens in lessons which keep you fastened to your desk. After dinner Joe and I went to the playing-field looking for a ball to kick, but instead we found Lorna Higgins and Jessie Watts. Jessie, her eyes like a deer's, was silent, but Lorna was so charged with anger or excitement or something that it exploded out of her when we were still twenty yards away.

'I want to talk to you!' she called to me.

I sighed. 'I can't stop you.'

'Just you,' she said. 'Nobody else.'

I stared at her. She was pale and her nose was pinched smaller than ever.

'Drop dead!' I said. 'Joe's my mate.'

'It's O.K., Dan,' Joe said. 'I'll clear off.'

'It's serious,' Lorna said, 'and I don't want anybody else to hear.'

Two lads out of my form walked past and gave me a low whistle and I glared at them. Then Joe followed them and little Jessie Watts walked over to the fence and pretended to be looking for something in the long grass.

'They're getting married!' Lorna shot at me.

'Who?'

'Who do you think? My dad and your mam!'

I sniffed. 'That's what you think!'

'It's today – this morning!' Her voice rose suddenly, tightening like a violin string. 'They'll *be* married by now!'

She meant it. It was incredible yet she believed it so strongly that there was a tumult inside her and I felt almost sorry for her.

'How do you know?' I asked.

'My dad told me and I never finished my breakfast. I couldn't. It would have choked me.'

I thought for a moment and then I snorted. 'My mother never said a word.'

She nodded. 'That's how they arranged it. They think you'll take it better if it's happened before you know. So they're going this morning with my Uncle Jim and somebody else ... is it your Aunt Nellie?'

'She's my mother's sister.'

'Well, she's going with them. My dad told me it was better for me not to go because you weren't going.' Her voice had been growing smaller. She paused and then sobbed and said, '*Me* go! I wouldn't go if they begged me!'

For a second or two I forgot my own anger. I was so confused by hers and embarrassed by her tears. She shook her head and wiped her eyes on the back of her hand.

'I just don't care what happens now,' she said.

I cared a lot.

'If you think I'm having your dad in our house, telling me ...' I started, but she looked at me.

There was a small fury inside her but she had it under control now and her voice when she spoke was fierce yet quiet.

'You don't know what you're talking about! My dad's the best there is and it was fine when there were two of us with me looking after him. Now he'll be looked after by *her*!'

There was so much venom in the last word that I could scarcely believe she was talking about my mother.

'Who?' I said. 'Who'll be looking after your dad?'

Her look hit me. '*Your mother!* Who'd you think?'

Now I was mad too. 'You ...' I started, but she wasn't listening to me. She was lonely with her own anger and resentment.

'I've heard people talking,' she went on, more quickly. 'I know what people think about it. She'll be coming into our house, running it and telling me what to do. Since my mother died nobody ... *nobody's* told me what to

56

do, but now *she's* coming and I know what she'll be like.'

My mind couldn't follow her; couldn't absorb the words and understand them quickly enough. She swung away from me, but I caught her arm and stopped her.

'You listen to me!' I growled at her.

'*No!* You listen to me! Your mother isn't living in our house! I'll kill her! I'll...'

'*Shurrup!*' I roared at her and she stopped and I knew that my anger was more frightening than hers.

'My mother's the best mother there is!' I said, quietly, yet thrusting the words at her, hammering them into her. 'And I don't want to live with your father. I don't like him. I once had a father – a real one – and I don't want somebody else trying to take his place. I've only got one father, even if he is dead, and don't you forget it!'

I was glaring at her and she was silent, holding her lips tightly shut. I'd never seen anything like the burning depths of her eyes.

'Lay off, Dan,' Joe said. 'You're hurting her.'

He'd come back and I hadn't seen him. My hand, still gripping her arm, was white and sculptured, and I opened it and walked away from her, back towards school. I heard Joe hurrying after me.

'What's up, Dan?' he said, sounding as if his troubles were greater than mine, and when I didn't answer because I couldn't he said again, 'What's up?'

I snorted the anger and tears out of my throat. 'You ought to have heard her! Telling me a lie like that!'

'Like what, Dan?'

I snorted again. 'Like my mother and her father got married this morning! That's what!'

'Flippin' heck!' he said, and then, after a thought, 'What's wrong with that, anyway? Mr Higgins is a

57

decent bloke. My mam says so, so he must be. So what's wrong with it?'

'It isn't true!' I snarled at him.

We walked on towards school, Joe silent now and thinking in his slow way.

'Married!' I said. 'She'd have told me! Wouldn't she, Joe?'

'I dunno. Mothers is funny sometimes.' He thought for a moment and then he said, 'If it is true, Dan, will you be called Dan Higgins?'

'It isn't true,' I said. 'I keep telling you. And my name's Rowley and it always will be. It'd be Rowley even if they did get married but they didn't. Look at Bill Thompson in Third Year. His mother's Mrs Joynson 'cos she got married again. Bill's dad's dead.'

'So's Mr Joynson,' Joe said. 'Leastways nobody ever sees him.' He glanced at me. 'Wonder why Lorna Higgins told you they were married if they weren't?'

'Dunno,' I said. 'Girls! They're all talk.' I stopped, certain that I couldn't live through the lifetime of the afternoon without knowing. 'I'm going home, Joe.'

'You'll be late and the prefects'll book you,' he said, and then, 'Flippin' heck! You playin' wag?'

I nodded. 'Tell old Jackson' – he was our Form Master – 'tell him I've got belly-ache so I've gone home.'

'That dinner was enough to give anybody belly-ache,' he said. 'He'll want a note in the morning, old Jackson will. Tell you what, Dan; I'll come with you.'

I stared at him. 'What for?'

He shrugged and was suddenly shy. 'You know. Case there isn't anybody in when you get home.'

'Don't talk daft!' I said. 'We might both get caught. You tell old Jackson.'

Then I punched him on the shoulder because I liked him and he grinned.

'I'll tell him, Dan. I'll make it the worst belly-ache

anybody ever had.' He thought for a moment. 'There's a soccer practice tonight and I don't want to miss that. You miss it and they may drop you for Saturday's match. Sprog's dead keen on practices.'

'Lot I care,' I said. 'You can tell him I got a belly-ache.'

'What about Wally Sinton?' he said. 'It's no good tellin' him lies 'cos he always knows.'

Joe's painstaking brain was thinking of everything while mine was saturated with uncertainty.

I sighed. 'Tell him I played wag, then. I'm off home.'

It was about half past one when I reached our house. I went in the back way, into the silence and emptiness my mother always left behind her. When she went out of the house she took with her the quality that turned it into a home. It was always the same, but that day it was even stronger. That day it seemed that a known way of life had ended. I wandered round, an ache in the pit of my stomach, and I went upstairs into her room. There was a hat on the bed and a pair of nylons draped over the back of a chair, but everything else was the same. I walked along the landing to my room and stopped in the doorway. The room was empty down to the cracked lino on the floor. Everything had been taken away, even the pictures of footballers I'd pinned to the wall. I was standing there, my numbed brain struggling to think, when I heard the front door open and my mother say, 'It'll only take me a minute or two to pack my things.'

I walked to the top of the narrow staircase and looked down at the door. She was in the hall, dressed finer than I'd ever seen her, and behind her was Walter Higgins, holding a suitcase. They both looked up at the same time, their eyes drawn by the disbelief in mine, and my mother said, 'Danny!'

There wasn't anything for me to say. I just stood there ·

and looked at them, at my mother in her finery and at Walter Higgins in a dark suit so new that the creases were still sharp in the trousers.

'Danny!' my mother said again. 'What are you doing here?'

'You know, don't you, son?' Walter Higgins said.

I nodded at that. 'Yes, Mr Higgins. I know you got married.'

My mother flushed. 'You must be playing truant, my lad! Everybody else is at school. You come down here this minute!'

'I won't!' I said.

She took a step towards the stairs but he caught her arm.

'You stay right where you are, son,' he said. 'If that's what you want.'

'Yes, Mr Higgins,' I said.

Already he was giving me permission, telling me what I could do. Very soon he'd be telling me what I couldn't do. I pushed my hands into my pockets and walked down the stairs and into the sitting-room and I sat in my dad's chair.

'You're going back to school,' my mother said, but her voice had lost its determination.

I was looking straight at Walter Higgins. 'You want to know who broke into your workshop? It was me!'

He sat opposite me and gave me a nod. 'Didn't make a very good job, did you? If a job's worth doing it's worth doing well. If you want to be a burglar you'd better learn the trade, son.'

'Don't call me "son". I'm not.'

He nodded again. 'I know. I had one.'

That doused my anger and I looked down at my hands and wondered if it was as bad for him with a dead son as it was for me with a dead father. Then, still looking down, I said, 'You going to tell the coppers?'

My mother sniffed. 'You talk like one of those children from Admiral Street. Anybody would think you were trying to make me ashamed.'

'I wish I was one of those kids from Admiral Street,' I said.

'If you were it wouldn't be anything to be ashamed of,' Walter Higgins said. 'And I'm not going to tell the coppers.'

'Why aren't you? They'd take me to court and I'd get sent away. Mugsy Jones told me.'

'So he knows about it, does he?' Walter Higgins said. 'If you'd told me he'd broken into my place I wouldn't have been at all surprised. And I don't want you to be sent away.'

'I do,' I said.

My mother made a wailing noise.

'Any fool can get himself sent away,' Walter Higgins said. 'All you need to do is go into town and throw a brick through the nearest shop-window and let a policeman catch you. You don't have to be clever to do that. They'll send you away all right and Walter Sinton'll soon find somebody else to take your place on the school team.'

I glanced up at him and found him looking straight at me.

'Your mother and me, Danny, we got married,' he said. 'We've had your room emptied and all your things taken to our house and put in a room just like they were here.'

'You can keep them,' I said. 'I'm not going.'

'Suit yourself, Danny,' he said.

'I will!' I stood up. 'I'm going back to school!'

They didn't try to stop me and I walked out of the house and back to school. Wally Sinton must have seen me coming because he was at the bottom of the stairs when I went in through the door.

We stood looking at each other for a moment and then he said, 'So your stomach's better? I was beginning to think you weren't going to be fit for Saturday's game. You let Mr Jackson know that you're here and then go to your class.'

I didn't play very well in the soccer practice at four o'clock. Sprog kept Joe and me shooting at goal while Jimmy Dodds and Brian Skelhorn sent in low passes from the wings. Joe was all right, but Joe always did everything right on a football pitch. His boot met every ball with a dull explosion that sent it bulleting into the net. I missed most of the balls and those I hit trickled away from my foot and barely reached the goal-line.

After a few minutes Sprog bellowed, 'What's up, young Rowley? Have you still got stomach-ache? Hit the ball as if you *hate* it!'

Hating was the thing I did best in those days. Jimmy Dodds sent the next ball over and as I ran at it I saw in it the face of Walter Higgins and I kicked it viciously.

Sprog watched the ball spinning in the bottom of the net and he said, 'Do that on Saturday, Rowley, and Cronton'll be sorry they're playing us.'

We changed after the practice and I went out of school with Joe. Just down the road going into Benton, Lorna Higgins and Jessie Watts were waiting for us. It was after five o'clock and they must have been waiting for more than an hour. Lorna stood facing me in the middle of the footpath. Determination, pinching her mouth and brightening her eyes, made her prettier than I'd ever seen her.

'Where are you going?' she asked me.

'Home! Where d'you think?'

'Where's home?' she asked.

A cunning, hurtful question and I couldn't answer it. Home was my mother in the kitchen, a bright cloth on the table, the smell of cooking.

'Your mother's at our house,' she said, 'and that's where you're supposed to go.'

'I'm off, Dan,' Joe whispered, as if he wanted nobody but me to hear him. 'See you in the morning.' He paused and I knew that he was thinking that he would never again be calling at our house for me.

'See you tonight,' he said. 'Call for me after tea.'

'You can go, Jessie,' Lorna said. 'You can't come with me tonight.'

Dismissed, Jessie glanced shyly at me, and followed Joe, who was already a hundred yards away, those bowed legs of his killing distance.

'Come on,' Lorna said to me. 'We're supposed to go *home*.'

She was sneering and I scowled at her.

'I'm supposed to please myself,' I said.

She sighed and stepped closer to me, so close that I could smell the clean, girl's smell of her, and she said, 'You don't like it because your mother's married my dad, do you? Well, I don't like it because my dad's married your old mother. I can't stop it and neither can you, but we don't have to like it and if we don't like it hard enough they may pack it up.'

She started to walk and I walked beside her.

'How do you mean?' I asked.

'They're worried about us,' she said in a whisper that drew me close to her. 'Least, my dad's worried about me so I suppose your mother's worried about you. We're both so important to them.' She was sneering again. 'You know how parents are. Putting the happiness of their children first and all that tripe. They want you and me to be happy and we aren't going to be. You've no idea how unhappy I can be when I want to.'

'And what will that do? You being unhappy?'

'Not me; both of us. If we're both miserable they'll be miserable, and then they'll start blaming each other and falling out and all that, and then they'll break it up and you can go back to your house.'

I listened to her, wrapped up in her conspiring, and we'd walked to the Chelford side of Benton and had reached the Higgins's house before I knew where we were.

I stopped. The house was a red-brick semi with a bow window upstairs and downstairs and a front garden with a wall.

'Home!' Lorna said sweetly.

7 Pop Burnett

Big fat Aunt Nellie was just leaving when we went into
the house; leaving and making a fuss about it as she
made a fuss about everything; talking, forgetting her
handbag, going to the wrong door, laughing till she
heaved. She gave me a pat on the head that made me
squirm and then she was gone, taking all her fuss and
tittering with her.

There was a large table in the dining-room, laid with
more good things than I'd seen since Christmas. Lorna
was walking round it, critical and silent, and then she
sniffed.

'No teaspoons!' she said. 'I wouldn't have forgotten
them.'

'Go and get them then,' her father said, and then to
me, 'Your room's second door on the right along the
landing. Want to have a look at it?'

'No,' I said.

My mother came in from the kitchen, looking flushed
and pretty and strange to me. Walter Higgins's eyes
followed her like a dog's.

'School all right, Danny?' she said to me, and then
before I could answer, 'Were you in trouble with Mr
Sinton? Have you seen the garden at the back? It's
lovely.'

'It's mine,' Lorna said in a small voice.

Her father gave her a thoughtful look. 'I don't remember you ever doing any work in it.'

'Lorna won't mind if Danny has a look at it,' my mother said. 'She can show him round after tea. Go and wash your hands, Danny. The bathroom's upstairs.'

I went, muttering to myself about the bathroom. The kitchen sink had always been good enough at home, but probably posh houses like Walter Higgins's didn't have kitchen sinks. The bathroom, when I found it, was big and pink. It had a pink bath tiled all round so that you couldn't see the dust underneath it, and a pink wash-basin and a pink W.C. I'd never seen a pink W.C. before. It was better than our cracked old white one at home.

I was a long time washing my hands and even longer finding how to flush the pink W.C. Then I went on to the landing and stopped outside the room which was to be mine. The door was open a little and I pushed it with my finger-tips. My football pictures were all there, Sello-taped to the wall, and my bed and my two boxes of treasure and my old chest of drawers with the same cracked mirror standing on it. It was my room all over again except that the wallpaper was new and there was a smell of fresh paint and the window looked out across fields to the hazy moors. I wanted to cry.

After a time I went downstairs. They were sitting round the table waiting for me, my mother pouring out cups of tea.

'We help ourselves to sugar,' Lorna said. 'That's the proper way of doing it.'

'Not for Danny,' my mother said. 'He never knows when to stop.'

That first meal in Walter Higgins's house was a night-mare. It takes more than fancy food to make a good meal : it takes friendship or affection. We had plenty of fancy food but little friendship and no affection. There was something electric in the air and there were the prickings of Lorna's soft sneers. Walter Higgins kept quiet. He listened and watched and he missed nothing.

He understood things about me my mother had never understood.

She talked. She said, 'What about school, Danny? Were you in trouble with Mr Sinton?'

I snorted. ' 'Course I wasn't!'

'Who made this jelly?' Lorna asked.

'Mm? The jelly?' my mother said. 'I did.'

Lorna nodded as if she'd known all the time. 'It's too floppy. I get it stiffer than this. I don't like it floppy.' She pushed her plate away.

'What did Mr Sinton say, Danny?' my mother asked.

'Say? Nothin',' I said. 'What did you expect him to say?'

'Is this *bought* cake, Dad?' Lorna asked.

His eyes came up slowly and my mother said, 'It is *not* bought cake. I made it yesterday.'

Lorna dropped the piece of cake she was holding on to her plate and said, 'It's heavy. It's like dough in the middle.'

I saw my mother's flush and I felt anger in my throat. I could have kicked Lorna Higgins. Instead I glared across the table at her and I said, 'You tryin' to make out my mother can't bake good cakes?'

She shrugged. 'I don't know, do I? All I know is that our cookery teacher would throw this into the bin.'

Her father pointed at her with his knife. 'One more remark from you, young lady, and you go to bed.'

Walter Higgins and I were on the same side and I didn't like it. I wanted to get away. I looked at my mother and said, 'Can I go out now?'

She glanced at Walter Higgins, but he was eating, studying the food on his plate. He knew when to say nothing. She nodded. 'When we've all finished. Where are you going?'

'Joe's,' I said.

When I escaped at last I ran all the way to Joe's. He

lived outside Benton, beyond the colliery, in an old farmhouse, a sprawling place roofed with heavy grey slates and built of bricks long since crumbled at the corners.

Mrs Carr must have seen me tearing up the lane because she was at the door waiting for me, with that quiet and concerned look of hers.

'Something frightened you, Danny?' she said.

I panted and shook my head.

'Then what are you running for?'

All I could do was shake my head again and she said, straight out, 'I'm pleased for your mother, Danny.'

I forgot that I was panting. 'Pleased?' I said.

She nodded. 'She's had her troubles – more than most. She's earned some happiness and she's got a good man. Walter Higgins has had his troubles, too.'

I was thinking that grown-ups stick together as if they all belong to the same union and then Joe came out, his face new-washed to shine his freckles.

'That was a beltin' goal tonight, Dan!' he said. He was embarrassed and afraid to look at me. 'Super! Nearly broke the net! Let's go for a good walk. It'll be like trainin'. Can we go for a walk, Mam?'

She smiled. 'You've already asked me an hour ago. I told you not to go too far. It still gets dark pretty early.'

We walked steadily round the edge of Benton, keeping away from the terrace streets. At first we were like two strangers, Joe shy, while I waited for him to ask me all about Walter Higgins and his house. He didn't ask me so at last I told him. I told him about my room and my football pictures and about the pink bathroom and the tea and Lorna's nastiness.

'She doesn't like it any more than I do,' I said. 'But she'd best lay off my mother!'

'Why should she like it?'

'Why should she? Don't talk daft! She's got my

mother to do the washing-up and the housework and everything. She's dead lucky!'

'Well, you've got her dad.'

I snorted. 'She can keep him!'

'But he'll stick up for you. Walter Higgins is O.K. A kid needs a dad to stick up for him against teachers and people. I'll bet Lorna Higgins thinks he's as good as you think your mam is.'

I was still considering this when we came to the new bungalows Sadler's were building among the trees and little hills at Thorley. Every one of them was a palace to me, bred as I was among terrace houses, and the kids who would soon live in them could only be kids for whom every day was Christmas.

At the corner of the unmade road that turned in to the estate was the little white-painted hut where Pop Burnett spent his nights guarding Sadler's property and plant.

Everybody in Benton knew Pop Burnett. He had a white beard stained brown with pipe smoke and every winter he washed it and became Father Christmas in one of Grimthorpe's big shops. The rest of the year he filled in selling matches and laces and waiting for the next winter. This night-watchman job was the best he had ever had. He lived alone in a house in Gaskin Street and he was one of the people my mother told me to keep away from. But I liked him because he knew how to talk to kids.

He was standing in the doorway of his hut, smoking his pipe and watching the sun finish its stint.

'Hi, Pop!' Joe called.

Pop drew his pipe out of his mouth, rattled the phlegm in his throat and said, ''Lo, there, Joe! Been playin' football lately? Bet you'll be playin' for Manchester United one o' these days. Bet you will.' His old eyes, blue as the sky, wandered to me. 'Edith Rowley's boy, ain't it? You another footballer?'

'He's super!' Joe said. 'He plays for our team and he's better than me.'

I was shaking my head when Pop said, 'Danny Rowley, ain't it? I mind you wanted a football for Christmas when you was two. Your mam brought you into t'shop. So you're a better footballer than young Joe Carr? You must be good.'

I shook my head again. 'Joe's the best there is.'

'Not yet he ain't,' Pop said. 'I mind when young Walter Sinton, him as is the schoolmaster, was the best there is. Saw him score the goal that beat Arsenal. You're lucky havin' him for schoolmaster. You ought to be a good team. Hear you're playin' that Cronton lot, Saturday.'

'Kick-off ten-thirty,' Joe said.

Pop pushed the pipe into his mouth. 'You'd best beat 'em, Saturday, Joe. A coupla goals'll do it. One each from you two lads. I'll be there watching.'

He glanced up, looking past us, and his mouth tightened on his pipe.

'Right now I'd best watch these two,' he muttered.

I turned round. Mugsy Jones and Snotty Smith were sauntering along the road, Snotty grinning. Mugsy winked at me and said, 'How's crime, kid?'

'You be off, Mugsy,' Pop said, his voice a wavering threat. 'Don't want no trouble from the likes o' you.'

Mugsy gave a long sigh. 'Charming! Me and Snotty we walk a couple of hundred miles 'cos we've got no bikes, all the way out to this dump to tell you how Mrs Yates says for you to call at her house in the morning for breakfast and that's all the thanks we get.'

'Why?' Pop asked. 'She gets me breakfast for me in me own house. Why've I to call at hers?'

'I don't know, do I?' Mugsy said. 'She didn't tell me. She just asked me would I tell you and my old man said if I didn't he'd kill me, and you know my old man.'

'You havin' me on, Mugsy?' Pop asked.

Mugsy sighed again and looked at Snotty. 'You try and do the old geezer a good turn and what do you get?'

'You ain't never done anybody a good turn in your life, Mugsy,' Pop said. 'You ain't never been a boy at all. You never played football like these two.'

'Football!' Mugsy growled. 'That's for squares. And I didn't come out here for a sermon from you, you old nit!'

·Snotty whistled. He was looking at the bungalows half-built among the trees.

'Bit of all right, eh, Mugsy?' he said. 'Going to be some brass round here.'

Mugsy looked, the dull anger dying out of his eyes. He nodded at the nearest bungalow, a double-glazed palace of stone and red cedar. 'Bet the bloke what's bought that don't get his hands dirty. Bet he never does a day's work.'

'That'll be the day,' Pop said slowly, 'when you do a decent day's work. It'll never happen. You ain't got the ... the moral fibre. You're as much use as fleas on a dog...'

'Put a sock in it!' Mugsy growled. 'You're always preachin'. Worse than a perishin' parson, you are.' He shuffled closer to Pop and then he looked past him, into the hut. 'Take a look at that lot! What you got there, Pop?'

Puzzled, Pop turned, not only his head but his body, too, as an old man does.

'What are you on about?' he muttered.

Mugsy chuckled. 'In that little snug o' yours. You do more than brew tea in there, you crafty old devil! I bet you swiped that lot!'

I could see white switch-covers and light-fittings and door-bells, all in stacked boxes.

'Bet that lot's worth a bit,' Mugsy said.

Pop turned back and his old eyes were sharp with anger. 'Them's Walter Higgins's electrics and he trusts me to look after them for him at night. Now you clear off. I may be gettin' on a bit, but I can still manage the likes o' you.'

Mugsy grinned at him, leaning forward and saying, 'Listen to Superman! You fancyin' your chance, Grandad?'

'He'd do all right,' I said, 'with me and Joe helpin' him.'

'You'd be on your own, Mugsy,' Joe said. 'Snotty couldn't fight our Elsie when she's asleep. Anyway, if we needed a bit of help it's on its way.'

Mugsy was still looking at me, his face full of thunder, and Joe nodded and said, 'You seen who's comin', Mugsy?'

Mugsy swung round. Robbo and Darkie Bates were walking up the lane.

He glowered at them, and when they turned into the unmade road he said, 'What do you two want?'

Robbo smiled. 'Don't want nothin', boy.'

'And we don't want no Niggers,' Mugsy growled.

Robbo took a quick step towards him but Pop, for all his years, was quicker. He caught Robbo's arm.

'You can stop that, you lads!' he said. 'Ain't havin' any trouble here. Nice folk, they are, what's comin' to live here and they wouldn't like it.'

Mugsy sneered. 'There isn't going to be any trouble, Pop.'

'Then you clear off,' Pop said.

'Come on, Mugsy,' Snotty said. 'This place is a dump. There isn't anything to do. Let's go into town.'

Snotty was afraid. There were now four of us and none of us feared Mugsy any longer. How can anybody fear a bully who's been knocked on to his backside by a younger boy?

'I was goin' anyway!' Mugsy said. 'I don't like the company.' He slouched away and at the corner he stopped and called, 'You best keep your eye on that stuff in your hut, Grandad! Some bad kids round here might pinch it!'

Pop watched him and slowly shook his head and I said, 'He's the one to talk about pinchin'!'

'You gonna be here all night by yourself, Mr Burnett?' Robbo asked.

Pop screwed up his eyes and looked carefully at Robbo. 'I'm here every night. I'm in charge. It's my job. Why are you askin'?'

Darkie's eyes did a wide roll. 'Wouldn't like it! Bet it ain't half spooky out here in the dark. No gaslamps.'

'I was just thinkin, Mr Burnett,' Robbo said, 'that it ain't right for you to be by yourself all night. You want somebody to stay with you? I bet my momma'd let me.'

'So'd mine,' Darkie said. 'But I wouldn't be no good. I'd be scared.'

'I bet lots of mommas in Admiral Street'd let their kids stay,' Robbo said. 'Somebody could stay with you every night, Mr Burnett. For company, like.'

Pop took his pipe out and left his mouth open. After a moment he said, 'That's thoughtful of you, lad; very thoughtful. But don't you worry none. I'm all right here.' He smiled. 'I may be gettin' on a bit but I can still look after myself. Kept myself fit, I have. When I was a lad I was as good a footballer as young Joe here.'

'Nobody's as good as Joe,' Darkie said.

'We'll see,' Pop said. 'Come Saturday I'll be at that match and we'll see how good Joe is.'

'I can't go,' Darkie said. 'Saturday, my momma makes me do the chores. Our Gloria does 'em Sunday.'

Pop was looking mistily at Joe and smiling, and Joe was shy. His feet had begun to shuffle uncomfortably.

I said, 'I'd best be getting home. It'll soon be dark.'

'Ay,' Pop said. 'Time for all you lads to be on your way home.'

I didn't hear him. I was thinking of home and remembering that I had none; that I lived now in Walter Higgins's house.

8 Football

Nothing much happened before Saturday. There wasn't anything else that could happen to me during those first days of loneliness and hopelessness in Walter Higgins's house. I suppose I was making adjustments. I hadn't intended to make any, yet unwillingly I was making many.

Everybody helped. Lorna helped most of all. Her resentment of my mother was such a force that at times it submerged my hatred and self-pity and drove me fighting mad in my mother's defence. My mother helped too. The shadows vanished from behind her eyes and she developed a child's fragile happiness which I had to protect. Walter Higgins, too, helped in his quiet way. He had a sedative quietness and with it a strength one could always feel.

On Friday during tea he said to me, 'The big match in the morning, isn't it?'

I grunted and he went on, 'Wouldn't mind coming along. I haven't seen a game in years.'

He'd never mentioned football to me before and I looked at him. 'Do you know anything about it?'

'About what?'

'Football. It's a game.'

He nodded. 'I seem to remember. I played it one time.'

'*You!*' I said, forgetting that he was a stranger who had taken my dad's place. 'I bet you did! Who did you

play for? Was it when you were a kid?' I couldn't believe that this big slow man had ever taken a pass in his
life. 'I bet it was when you were a kid and it was with a
tin can. That isn't football. Football's an ... an *art*!
Wally Sinton says so and he ought to know.'

'He'll know all right,' he said.

'My dad was a super footballer!' Lorna cut in. 'He was
a better footballer than you'll ever be!'

I grunted. 'So what?'

Anger was bruising her cheeks again. 'He was a better
footballer than your old mother's a cook!' she flamed.

Walter Higgins just said, 'Go to your room, girl,' but
my mother said, 'No.'

She was shaking. her head. 'No, Walter. She may be
right. I don't claim to be a very good cook.'

'It's her rudeness,' he said.

She smiled. 'Her rudeness doesn't hurt me. It hurts her
more than anybody.'

He looked at her for a moment or two and then he
bent to his plate again. That's how Lorna helped me. All
my bitterness had to be used against her and I had none
left for Walter Higgins.

'I'll go and watch the match in the morning,' he said.
He looked at my mother. 'How about it, love?'

She shook her head. 'Not me. I'm too busy learning
how to cook.'

'Then I'll go,' he said. 'Wouldn't mind learning a bit
about football.'

I watched him suspiciously. I'd known him long
enough to recognise that the twinkle in his eyes was the
reflection of some secret joke. All his jokes were secret
from me.

Wally Sinton had told our team to go to bed early that
Friday night so I went early. I switched the light off and
pulled my head in like a tortoise and said my prayers. In
the dark I might have been in my own room back at

home. My mother thought I'd stopped saying my prayers two years before when my nightly broadside of praying had failed to keep my dad alive. But I still prayed. I was scared to stop. I was afraid that if I stopped praying I'd have no insurance against further tragedy.

So I said my private prayers that night in the darkness under the bedclothes, whispering them so that only God could hear. There were kids at school who said there was no God; that there couldn't be because nobody had ever proved the truth of God. But nobody had ever proved the untruth of God so I kept on saying my prayers.

I prayed that night that we should beat Cronton the next day and that I should score one goal and Joe another. I prayed for my mother — I'd never stopped doing that even when she became somebody else — but I didn't pray for Walter Higgins. I'd prayed many a time for him to die but I'd stopped. It didn't work. Praying for death for the living was as much use as praying for life for the dying.

I was at school at ten o'clock the next morning with an ache in my stomach where my breakfast should have been. Sprog was already in the changing-room, as nervous as a rabbit, fussing with a new ball and trying to find some confidence to pass to us. I could hear the deep rumble of broken voices from the other changing-room and I wondered if the Cronton boys felt as weak and defeated as I felt.

It was a fine morning with a memory of winter still in the breeze. The air stung through shirt and shorts when I trotted with the others on to the field.

'Good crowd,' Jimmy Dodds said. 'I like a crowd. It makes me play better. Beltin' crowd, Paddy! They'll be cheerin' for us.'

Paddy Cleary's father and grandfather had both been born in England yet they had bred into him an Irish brogue. He had a bull-dog nose and chin under his red hair.

'Wish they were playin' for us,' he said. 'I do so. Have you seen what's comin' on to the pitch?'

I turned and for the first time saw the Cronton team, every boy in it a giant.

'Flippin' heck!' Joe Carr breathed. 'We're playin' against the teachers!'

The Cronton lads filled their bright red shirts with muscular bodies. They started shooting-in at the other end of the pitch and there was a purposeful authority about them and a confidence that made me feel like a kid.

Paddy Cleary chuckled. 'One thing's for sure, Danny,' he said to me. 'You and young Joe'll be O.K. Keep in the long grass and they'll never find you.'

Then Sprog's whistle shrilled, and the captains were shaking hands and stamping their feet, and the Cronton captain was winning the toss. We had to play into the breeze.

We lined up. One of the Cronton forwards, a six-foot god in a red shirt, looked at Joe and then at me and he laughed and I wanted to kick him in the teeth.

'They must be juniors!' he said. 'It's a shame to take the money!'

I snarled at him. 'See who scores the goals, big head!'

Then Sprog's whistle went off like a falling bomb and Joe tapped the ball to me, and the big Cronton forward, still laughing, charged into me, flattened me and ran over me. I sat up slowly, mad and ashamed. I could see the crowd wavering on the touchline and Walter Higgins with Lorna, her face a pink patch of derision. Pop Burnett was shouting, *'Foul! Foul! Ref!'*

It was no foul. It was Goliath charging David before he'd loaded his sling, but it was no foul. Football's a battle, and in battle bodies are flattened as mine had been. I stood up slowly. The big Cronton forward was somewhere near our penalty area, still with the ball at his feet, and he was making straight for Bob Morris, intent on destruction. Bob was the quietest lad on our team and the best part of our defence. He had a squat broad body, hard with bone and muscle, and he was not built to be destroyed. He planted himself and the Cronton forward ran into him and I heard the clash from forty yards away, like a steamboat running into a rock. The Cronton boy wilted and staggered back, hugging his ribs, while Bob, unmoved and immovable, stood with the ball at his feet. He booted it thoughtfully up the field and Joe Carr's foot touched it with a spell that tamed it and made it his. He sped forward a few yards and slipped the ball to Jimmy Dodds, and another Cronton giant, like a bull, floored Jimmy, took the ball on, brushed Paddy Cleary aside and shot.

Pop Burnett was screaming, 'Foul!' and groups of kids were chanting, 'Dirty Cronton!'

Sprog's whistle blew for a corner.

Corners were bad for us. Any ball in the air was beyond the reach of our midget team. This corner sailed across the goalmouth and a Cronton head, unopposed, nodded it over the bar.

That was how the game went on. There were three corners against us in the first ten minutes and we were in the Cronton half only once before half-time. We weren't playing against footballers. We were playing against juggernauts.

I could see Wally Sinton on the touchline, standing beside the Cronton headmaster in duty rather than friendship. The Cronton headmaster was wearing a black overcoat and a black Homburg hat and he looked like an undertaker waiting for a funeral.

The crowd was quiet now. Even our own kids were quiet, huddled together in tight groups, preparing themselves for humiliation. Already the cowards among them were leaving. There was nobody to shout the right words to us.

The next ten minutes went badly. Cronton should have scored four goals but they were playing with us, talking to each other and laughing and rushing through our defence one at a time so that they had neither subtlety nor cohesion; they were not a team. We were packing our goal-mouth and in all that time I kicked the ball once, my desperate boot sending it soaring almost to the half-way line.

'Keep it on the ground!' somebody shouted.

I looked across at the touchline.

'Keep it on the ground!' he shouted again, and I couldn't believe it. It was Walter Higgins.

'What's *he* know about football?' I snarled.

Wally Sinton was with him, saying a few quick earnest words, and I saw Walter Higgins nod and Wally Sinton go back to his post beside the Cronton headmaster, and it occurred to me then that Wally's fight was harder than ours.

It was while I was thinking about this that Cronton scored. My kick had driven back the tide for only a few seconds. A Cronton foot hit the ball clumsily and pushed it to another Cronton player and then their forwards were rushing over us again. I never knew how the goal was scored or who scored it. I knew that their charge broke against Bob Morris and flowed round him and that there was a goalmouth scramble I was too weary to reach. I saw desperate stabbing feet all round the ball and then it was driven into the net and the Cronton players were hugging each other while Billy Sprunt, our goalkeeper, was red-faced and cursing under his breath.

A few minutes later it was half-time and I was trudging unwillingly to where our boys were gathering round Sprog.

Joe Carr said to me, 'We could eat this lot! Flippin'

heck! There isn't a footballer among 'em!'

'Right, Joe!' somebody said.

It was Walter Higgins, out on the pitch where spectators were trespassers, and Wally Sinton was with him, his face white and his eyes angry.

'Are you afraid of them?' he asked.

There was a growled denial.

'Then why are you playing as if you've never seen a football in your lives before?'

'They're so big, sir,' Jimmy Dodds said. 'You can't play football against that lot.'

He was outraged and angry and Wally Sinton looked at him a long moment and then said, 'How do you know, Jimmy? You haven't begun to try yet.'

He swung on me. 'How long have you been a fullback, Rowley? Your job's to make goals and score them. You too, Carr. You're trying to play it their way and you aren't big enough. Play it your own way. Short quick passes and don't be caught in possession.'

'They'll still flatten us, sir,' Paddy Cleary said and he was grinning. 'They will so. We aren't chicken, but we can't play against steam-rollers.'

'They won't flatten you after you've passed the ball,' Wally Sinton said.

'Not while Sprog's referee,' he added.

Wally Sinton turned to Walter Higgins. 'What do you think, Walter? How should they play it?'

Walter Higgins nodded slowly. 'Like you say. Ball on the ground. They're taller than you. Find the open spaces and run into them. Big as they are, they can't fill the whole pitch, so there'll always be spaces. Use the ball. Let it do the work for you.'

I was staring at him. 'What do you know about it?' I asked, and I wasn't being cheeky. I couldn't believe that lumbering Walter Higgins had ever played a game of football in his life.

'More than you're ever likely to know, Rowley,' Wally Sinton said in his snapping voice. 'So listen to him. I can't shout at you so listen to Mr Higgins, all of you, and play as he says.'

'Time!' Sprog said.

Cronton kicked off for the second half. As I waited for the whistle I could feel the breeze on my back, freezing the dampness round my waist.

I don't remember the kick-off. The first thing I remember is the ball at my feet and wondering how it got there and no Cronton giant within twenty yards. I ran forward and glanced up for a glimpse of Joe Carr, forgotten and unnoticed, at the corner of the Cronton penalty area. I stabbed the ball towards him and a Cronton boy, rushing at me to destroy me, grunted and swerved away.

'Nicely played!' Walter Higgins called and I felt a little throb of pleasure, as if Wally Sinton had called.

Joe was streaking for goal. He sent one Cronton fullback floundering the wrong way with a sway of his hips, and a swerve took him round the other and then he was alone in front of goal. I don't think many people saw the shot. Joe was running at top speed, his head down and his shoulders forward, when the ball blasted away from his foot and was bulging the net before the Cronton goalie had moved.

The yell from the crowd almost deafened me and it brought back most of the cringing kids who had tried to escape humiliation. They came pouring on to the field, shouting as loudly as those who'd stayed. I could see Lorna Higgins clapping and next to her Jessie Watts, jumping up and down. I found I was laughing.

Joe said to me, 'Super pass, that, Dan! Our Elsie could have scored off a pass like that. I'll try and give you one.'

That goal took all the swaggering confidence out of

Cronton. They still charged about but now, instead of charging at us, they were charging after us. We remembered what Wally Sinton had told us and we slipped the ball away before a tackle crushed us. If anybody held the ball too long Walter Higgins's voice cut across the field, 'Pass!' so that very soon I was passing when he told me to.

For the next twenty minutes we played football while Cronton floundered, but we scored no more goals. Cronton were desperate and worried and they barricaded their goalmouth with a solid line of players every time we attacked.

'Another pass like that last one, Dan,' Joe whispered to me while we waited for a goalkick. 'What a flippin' defence! They've got ten fullbacks.'

The goalkick sailed high overhead, beyond the halfway line, and Bob Morris stolidly retrieved it.

'Space, lad!' Walter Higgins was calling.

I saw him point, just a quick stab of his finger, at the emptiness to the left of the Cronton penalty area and I ran into it. When I turned there was Joe slipping the ball to Jimmy Dodds and running round him to take the return pass and streaking along, a tiny magician, until Walter Higgins called, 'Pass!'

I knew before Joe's foot hit it that the ball would be mine. I saw it slanting across the goalmouth, scorching the crushed grass, and I ran on to it. I don't remember shooting. All I remember is Paddy Cleary thumping my back while Jimmy Dodds hung round my neck. I remember, too, the roar, like a wild sea, that battered against my ears, and Lorna Higgins clapping and Jessie Watts quietly smiling and Walter Higgins nodding.

'Super!' Joe said. 'Best goal this season!'

'It was so!' said Paddy Cleary.

'It was the pass,' I said. 'Lorna Higgins could have scored off a pass like that.'

Joe blushed and turned away and Sprog's whistle blew a victory blast to end the game.

As Joe and I walked off the field I saw Walter Higgins crossing in front of us with Lorna and Jessie Watts. He gave me a nod and said, 'Nicely played, lad,' but I was looking at Jessie Watts, seeing her as if for the first time. She was gazing at me, her eyes big and liquid, and I felt as important as a pop-singer. It was a good feeling that made me glow inside.

Sprog was waiting for us in the changing-room, hopping about like a crazy kid. Wally Sinton was standing there, quietly watching, and the satisfaction in his eyes was enough for us.

'You did well, Rowley,' he said to me. 'It was a good goal.'

'It was Carr's pass, sir,' I said.

'It was your shot,' he said.

I remembered then that it was Walter Higgins's call that had triggered my foot. I couldn't remember the shot, but I knew that Walter Higgins, calling 'Shoot!' had fired it.

'I didn't know he'd ever played football,' I said.

'Walter Higgins? He was one of the best half-backs I ever had behind me.'

'Who did he play for, sir?' I asked.

'Benton. So did I. His father made him learn a trade instead of going into first-class football.'

Somebody snorted. It was Paddy Cleary, listening to us in the noise of the changing-room.

'I know what I'd rather do!' he said. 'Play for Everton or learn a trade! I do so!'

'Footballers weren't glamour-boys when I was a lad, Cleary,' Wally Sinton said. 'You'll make a fine glamour-boy. In fact, you're a bit of a glamour-boy now.'

We all laughed, Paddy harder than any of us.

84

9 Robbery

I stayed in Walter Higgins's house all that Saturday afternoon, in my own room, sorting out my pictures of footballers. Lorna was having Jessie Watts in after tea to listen to her tapes of pop-singers. Joe was calling for me and we were going for a walk. There wasn't much to do at night in Benton if you didn't like taped pop-singers or you didn't want to watch telly programmes chosen by grown-ups.

Tea was a peaceful meal. Lorna was behaving herself, corking her bitterness up because she was afraid her dad would retaliate by banning Jessie's visit. So the atmosphere round the table was as friendly as the food on it. I liked the food but not the friendliness.

'I'd have thought you and Joe were too tired to go walking,' my mother said to me. 'After playing football this morning, I mean.'

I snorted. 'We've got over that. Anyway, I wasn't tired. You only get tired when you lose.'

Walter Higgins smiled. My mother said, 'But Joe's got a long walk here. He'll be tired before you start.'

'He's coming on his bike,' I said. 'He got it for his birthday.'

'Can you ride a bike?' Walter Higgins asked me.

''Course I can.'

'But you never had one,' my mother said. 'How did you learn? I've told you the roads are dangerous.'

'Aw!' I groaned. 'I learned on other kids' bikes. Anybody can ride a bike.'

'Jessie can't,' Lorna said. 'She tried once on mine and she fell off.'

'Every lad ought to have a bike,' Walter Higgins said. He chewed and swallowed. 'That's how he learns road sense.'

'Or breaks his neck,' my mother said.

We'd only just finished when Joe arrived, flying head-down up the road. When I went outside he had pushed his bike up the path and was propping it carefully against the house.

'O.K., Dan,' he said. 'Let's go that walk.'

He was looking past me into the house, afraid of Lorna yet hoping to see her. We set out towards Thorley, talking about the morning's game, and we met Jessie Watts, as slim as a pole in her jeans, on her way to listen to Lorna's tapes. She walked right out into the road to avoid us and as we passed she gave me a quick smile and a doe-like glance that caught me looking at her.

Joe said, 'She's daft.'

For some reason this irritated me and I growled, 'Why?'

' 'Cos she never talks. A girl who never talks must be daft. Our Elsie never talks to me, but you ought to hear her with other people.'

'I've heard her. How do you know it isn't your Elsie that's daft?'

He thought about this. 'Our Elsie *is* daft. She's daft about lads. I suppose all girls are daft.'

' 'Cept Lorna Higgins,' I said.

He blushed. Then after a moment he said, 'What's it like living with her, Dan? What's she like?'

'Dead rotten. She's worse than daft. She's nasty.'

'She doesn't look nasty,' he said.

Suddenly I was angry with him. He'd felt her bitterness and her scorn, and he accepted them and could find no fault in her.

'Shurrup about her!' I said. 'You don't know what she's like. You ought to hear how she talks to my mother. You don't know what you're talking about, so stick to football.'

We talked football after that until we were well out in the country. Then we watched the sheep packing themselves into one corner of a field for the night and afterwards we went into Long-Wood, where it skirts the Thorley road, and threw stones at the rooks' nests in the highest trees. When we came to the road again, Joe said, 'I'd best be going back, Dan. It'll soon be dark.'

Shadows were stealing through the trees and already the first star was out.

'So what?' I said. 'I'll go back when I want to.'

He looked at me, puzzled. 'My dad told me not to be late.'

'I haven't got a dad. I've only got Walter Higgins and he doesn't count. Anyway, I wanted to go and see old Pop Burnett. He was at the match this morning.'

I stopped. His head had turned and he was listening, and I listened with him. Somebody was running, his feet beating out an urgent alarm on the road, and Joe grabbed my arm. Then Hector Robinson came racing in that long loose style of his round the bend at the far end of Long Wood. He came up with us and kept straight on and we dashed after him. He wasn't even panting.

'What's up, Robbo?' I shouted at him.

He shook his head. 'Bad! Blood out of his mouth.'

I glanced at Joe and he said, 'Whose mouth?'

'On his back,' Robbo said. 'Out of his head, too. Blood.'

I caught his arm and hung on and made him stop.

'What's up with you?' I growled at him. 'You seen a ghost or something?'

'No ghost,' he said. 'Pop Burnett.'

'What about him?'

'I told you, boy. On his back in that hut of his and

87

blood coming out of him.' Robbo's eyes, normally still and calm, were now wide and staring. 'I'm off to get the scuffers.'

'You mean he's had an accident?' I asked.

His eyes opened, wider than ever. 'Accident! He's been raided. They've pinched the stuff that was stored in Pop's hut and they've done him.'

My hand was still holding Robbo's arm and I looked down at the pattern of scratches on the back of it.

'You on your own, Robbo?' I asked.

'You see anybody with me?' he said. 'Darkie, he'd got to stay in 'cos his uncle was comin' from Birmingham. Charlie's momma won't let him out 'cos she heard about that fight me and you was in, and she's scared of him fightin' white kids. Ain't no other kids, so I thought I'd go and see old Pop. He was sort of good to talk to, was Pop.'

' "Was"?' Joe said. 'You mean he's dead?'

'Dunno,' Robbo said. 'He looked dead to me, but I ain't never seen anybody dead except on telly and they're only actin' dead. You ever seen anybody dead?'

The last time I'd seen my dad, death had passed me, coming into his room as I was leaving it, and I hadn't recognised it.

'Why don't you find a house and ask them to telephone?'

I said to Robbo. 'You'll be ages getting to Benton. And what about an ambulance? There are some houses round here.'

Quietly, he said, 'You want to try bein' coloured, and goin' and askin' white people can you use the telephone. You want to try it, boy.'

Suddenly I was angry at the stupidity of grown-ups. 'Well, I'll ask them! They can't say I'm coloured. Where's a house?'

'Back along there round the bend.'

I started to run.

'How do you know it'll have a telephone?' Joe asked, coming up alongside me.

'I don't. We can find out, can't we?'

We turned the corner and plunged back into daylight after the half-night under the trees of Long Wood and right away I saw the house. It had once been a country-man's cottage, but now a townsman had taken it and covered it with stucco and new paint and put great sheets of glass where little windows ought to have been.

'Telephone,' I said, pointing at the wires.

We ran up the path. The door was dark oak, studded with imitation nail-heads, and I hit it with my fist. I could hear the electronic crackle of television voices and I waited for a few moments and hit the door again.

It was opened by a short man with angry, watery eyes. His mouth opened, but before he could speak I said, 'Can we use your telephone, please, Mister? Some-body's raided Sadler's and beaten up Pop Burnett.'

'Sadler's?' he said. 'Where's Sadler's?'

All I could think of was Pop lying in his hut with the blood still running out of him and I knew that there was none to spare in his old dried-up body.

'Where they're building the new bungalows!' I said, almost shouting. 'We've got to get an ambulance quick!'

'Ambulance!' he snorted. 'You clear off out of here quick or it's the police you'll get! I know your game! You phone the ambulance, then you disappear, and I'm stuck with the job of explaining. You clear off!'

I couldn't believe it. I said, 'There's . . .' but he backed inside and slammed the door and I was left staring at the imitation nail-heads.

'It's 'cos I was here,' Robbo said.

I gave an angry growl. 'Don't be daft! It's 'cos he's a mean old devil!'

I kicked the door so hard that the sound of it went

drumming through the house and I turned and ran, Joe and Robbo chasing after me.

'You shouldn't have done that!' Joe panted.

I heard the man's voice come snarling after us and I said, 'I'd do it again, harder! What's he care about Pop?'

We turned into the lane and a new idea flashed into my mind. 'The hut! I bet there's a phone in the hut, isn't there, Robbo?'

'Dunno,' he said. 'All I saw was Pop with blood comin' out of him and all them things that had been pinched.'

'If there is a phone,' Joe said, 'it won't be any good. The gang would cut the wire. That's what gangs always do.'

We dashed, panting, round another bend and there were the half-built bungalows sinking into the shadows among the trees, and Pop's hut with telephone wires I could see from fifty yards away. I surged forward faster than ever and then, a few feet from the door, uncertainty stopped me, my heart thumping in my throat until I thought I would choke. Behind me Joe and Robbo stood so close that I could feel the heat from their bodies.

I crept to the door of the hut. The first thing I saw was Pop's pipe lying on the floorboards in a scatter of black ash. Then I saw Pop. He was sitting on the floor, leaning forward and weakly holding his cracked head in both hands.

'You O.K., Pop?' I whispered.

He looked up very slowly. ''Lo, you lads. That was a good goal you scored, son.'

Joe and Robbo followed me into the hut.

'Who was it, Mr Burnett?' Robbo asked.

'Who was what, lad?'

'Who hit you?'

Pop felt his bleeding scalp again. 'Summat must 'a fell on me. I mind I'd done a tour round the bungalows and I came back and it was gettin' dark. I put my hand up to switch the light on and summat fell on me and caught me a fair old wallop. I came to a few minutes since and I didn't know where I was.'

'It wasn't anything fell on you, Mr Burnett,' Robbo said. He pointed at the emptiness behind Pop. 'You been raided.'

Pop turned painfully round and looked at the floor. 'All Walter Higgins's stuff!' he said, as if to himself. 'All gone. Would you credit it? Like a bank robbery it is.'

He started to climb to his feet and we helped him. He flopped about like a puppet with broken strings, and we lowered him carefully on to the wooden chair beside the bench. Then I saw the telephone. I picked it up.

'Ay,' Pop said. 'Get the police, lad.'

'You dial nine-nine-nine,' Joe said. 'I've seen them do it on the telly.'

I dialled and a woman's brisk voice answered.

'She's asking me which service I want,' I growled at Joe. 'Marvellous, isn't it? She must think I want a bus! All I want's the police.'

'Police!' the brisk voice twanged in my ear. 'Where are you calling from?'

'Sadler's,' I told her. 'You know ... where they're building at Thorley. There's been ...

'One moment, please,' she said.

'All the stuff was Walter Higgins's,' Pop was muttering. 'He won't like it.'

I snorted. 'I want to see his face when they tell him.'

'You sound glad,' Joe said to me, scowling. 'He was on our side this morning.'

'Police!' a man's voice said in my ear.

'There's been a burglary,' I told the telephone. 'Robbo discovered it and Pop Burnett's been beat up. Joe and me came back with Robbo and I'm phoning for the police.'

'And who're you?' the policeman asked.

'Danny Rowley.'

'And where are you?'

'Thorley. In Sadler's hut where they're building the bungalows. Somebody's pinched all Walter Higgins's switches and things, and laid Pop Burnett out, and he's bleeding.'

'You stay right where you are, son,' the policeman said. 'We'll have somebody there in five minutes.'

'What about an ambulance?' I said.

'Take it easy,' he said, and I realised that I'd been shouting. 'The ambulance'll be on its way before you've put the phone down.'

But I didn't put it down. I looked at Joe and I said, 'I'm going to tell Walter Higgins. Pass that phone book.'

'He isn't going to like it,' Pop said. 'And I told him I'd look after the stuff.'

It was Lorna who answered. I made my voice deep and posh and said, 'I would like to speak to Mr Higgins, please.'

'All right,' she said, disappointment dripping out of her voice.

Then Walter Higgins came and I said, 'This is Danny Rowley,' and I told him in a rush. 'And all your stuff's been pinched,' I ended. 'Will it make you bankrupt?'

'Ever heard of insurance?' he said. 'I'll get the police.'

'I've already got them. And I've got an ambulance for Pop. They're both on the way.'

'Good lad. How is Pop?'

'Hurt bad. He's got a big cut in his head.'

'Let me tell him,' Pop whispered, putting his hand out for the phone.

'I'll come in the car,' Walter Higgins said.

I put the phone down and for some reason I was panting.

'He's on his way,' I said to Pop. 'You can tell him then.'

He wiped his hand over his face. 'He isn't going to like it. He can be tough, can Walter. Doesn't get in a flaming temper like most men. When he's in a temper he's just cold and quiet and quick.'

'It isn't your fault,' I told him. 'You aren't supposed to be able to fight an armed gang. Anyway, what are you worryin' about? Walter Higgins'll be O.K. Ever heard of insurance?'

The police and the ambulance came together five minutes later, their headlights cutting swathes out of the darkness, and who should be the first to walk into the hut but Detective Sergeant Garside, the sour-faced staring copper who couldn't even solve the break-in at Walter Higgins's workshop. He was followed by the young copper in uniform who'd caught me smashing gaslamps. I knew only two coppers in all Benton and they both had to come.

Behind them were two ambulance men. They wanted to carry Pop out on a stretcher but he wouldn't let them. He walked out with one of them helping him, and as he went he said, 'You won't keep me long at that hospital, will you, son? I've got to be back here tomorrow night.'

'Sure, Dad,' the ambulance man said and winked at me.

The detective followed them and that left us with the uniformed copper, who took off his cap and rubbed his bristly head and said, 'Trouble for somebody.'

'For Pop,' Joe said.

'And Walter Higgins,' I said.

Robbo kept quiet. For ten minutes now he'd been standing in a corner where the shadows were deepest, as still as a rabbit before a stoat.

The detective came back. 'He's no help,' he said, speaking to himself. 'Never saw such a thing. Still thinks something fell on him.'

He looked at me, then at Joe and finally at Robbo, at

each of us for a long time, staring as he'd done that day in Wally Sinton's room.

He looked back at me. 'Who found him?'

I kept quiet. He could make me more stupidly stubborn than anybody I ever knew.

'I asked you who found him,' he said.

'It was me,' Robbo said, and his voice was gruff and defensive.

The copper turned his head slowly to look at him. 'You was it? And what was he doing when you found him?'

'He wasn't doin' nothin'. He was . . .'

'You mean he was sitting in that chair?' the detective said. 'Or looking out the window?'

He was setting traps again and I said, 'He means he was doing nothing. That's what he told you. Pop was lying on the floor and he was unconscious.'

'You seem to know all about it,' the detective said. 'Were you with this coloured boy?'

I shook my head and he glanced at the constable and said, 'A lot of help we're going to get from this lot.'

'You've had plenty already,' Walter Higgins said.

He was standing in the doorway, filling it, and we'd never heard him come. For once I was glad to see him.

The detective swung round. 'How do you mean?'

'I mean that these are the boys who reported the theft and maybe saved Pop Burnett's life. He's too old a man to be knocked about.' Walter Higgins was looking straight at the detective, straight into his eyes. 'These lads have done their share.'

I could have cheered. Walter Higgins had reduced that copper even more than Wally Sinton had done. I glanced at the constable and caught a smile on his face. He winked at me and I was sure that he was cheering inside just as hard as I was.

10 Trap

I was late the next morning yet I was first up. My mother had never been one for staying in bed before we went to live at Walter Higgins's house, but she was late that morning. I lay in bed for a long time, wide awake and watching the sunshine fill the room with spring, and then I got up and washed and dressed and went downstairs and into the garden at the back. There wasn't a whisper to disturb the Sunday quiet. I'd never known a Sunday morning like that one. There was a holiness about which never could have been felt in the daily din of our old street.

Walter Higgins kept his garden trim. There was a square lawn with an edge so straight he must have ruled it, and a border where the soil looked as if it had been sieved and combed. I strolled round the lawn and then I tried some hand-stands on it, and at the second go I got my legs straight up. Then a window slid open and I fell into the roses.

'Don't you mess up our garden, Danny Rowley!' Lorna called to me.

She was leaning out of her bedroom window, still in her pyjamas, her hair gripped in curlers, and I said to her, 'Get lost!' Then, standing up, I looked at her again and I laughed.

I'd never seen her with her skull clamped in tight curls and I laughed until my stomach ached.

'What's so funny?' she asked.

I pointed at her. 'You! You want to look in a mirror. I wish Joe Carr could see you with your hair like that. I bet he'd run a mile.'

She dodged back and slammed the window on my laughter.

I enjoyed that morning. I enjoyed the novelty of a house where nothing blocked the sunshine and where other people's kids couldn't play outside your front door. Walter Higgins was out most of the time with the police, listing the stuff that had been stolen. My mother was working in the house and Lorna helped her because her dad had told her to. I could feel Lorna's resentment even in the garden and I could picture her at the sink, her mouth droopy and bitter, and her anger ready to consume her. I couldn't help but worry about what her anger might do to my mother. I knew that my mother was the best and I knew that Walter Higgins thought so too. Watching him look at her made me burn inside.

Sunday dinner was a quiet meal, but at the end of it Lorna's bitterness exploded out of her. I was sitting opposite her and the dark smouldering in her eyes had been making me uneasy for some time.

Walter Higgins finished his pudding, pushed his plate away and said, 'I enjoyed that, Edith. Best meal I've had in ages.'

Lorna gave a little strangled moan and then screamed so fiercely that I was knocked backwards in my chair, '*It wasn't! It was no good! She can't cook!*' Then she sprang up and rushed out of the room.

I was scared. Big bullying lads like Mugsy Jones couldn't scare me, but Lorna scared me that day. It was the first time I'd seen the release of savagery that most of us manage to keep bottled up.

Walter Higgins, his face pale and angry, stood up and my mother looked at him and said, 'Leave her, Walter.'

She was the calm in the whirlwind and her calmness

quietened him. He sat down and watched her as she steadily finished her pudding. Then she stood up and walked out of the room and I heard her going upstairs.

Walter Higgins glanced uneasily at me and I knew that, if I was scared, he was confused.

'Queer creatures, girls,' he growled. 'Can't understand them.'

I said nothing because there were so many things I didn't understand. All I knew was that Lorna had frightened me so much that I wasn't even angered by her bitterness.

We sat and looked at our empty plates, at the sunshine on the road outside, until at last he said, 'You going out today?'

'Joe's coming,' I said.

He nodded. 'Good lad, Joe. Ought to make a name for himself with his football.'

'You didn't,' I said, remembering that he'd never told me, had let me think he didn't know the game.

'Things were different then,' he said. 'Football wasn't a career when I was a lad. It was a game you played until you were too old and then you were left with nothing to do.'

'Wally Sinton wasn't.'

'His parents could afford to send him to college, and he'd the brains to do the work and carry on with football at the same time.'

Then my mother came back with Lorna. I'd never seen my mother look so wise or smile so sadly. Lorna's face was blotchy red and she kept her head down to hide her puffy eyes.

'Lorna and I have had a talk,' my mother said. 'I think she understands that I'm not trying to be as good as her mother. I'm just doing the best I can.'

Lorna glanced under her eyelids at me, like a trapped and beaten tiger. 'A lot of help you were!' she whispered.

'What's that supposed to mean?' Walter Higgins asked.

I knew what it meant. I knew that she expected me to live on bitterness, to be as nasty with my mother as she was, to brew hatred in my heart. I hated what Walter Higgins had become, but I could no more hate him than I could hate a cart-horse.

'It means,' my mother said, 'that these two had planned to make us all so unhappy that we'd break up.'

Walter Higgins was still staring at her, his mouth open, when somebody rang the doorbell and he jumped up and said, 'I'll go.' I knew that he was glad to get out of the room.

But I had to stay there, waiting and listening and not letting my eyes wander towards my mother, until he came back with Darkie Bates behind him. My mother gasped. It was the first time she'd ever had a coloured boy in her house.

'What . . .' she started, but I cut her off.

'He's a mate o' mine!' I said, glaring, and then I turned to Darkie, whose eyes were flashing like beacons from my mother to Walter Higgins and back to my mother.

'What's up?' I asked him.

He cleared his throat and I saw his Adam's apple bob. 'It's Robbo. They've taken him away.'

'Who's Robbo?' my mother asked.

His eyes swivelled towards her but I said to him, 'Who's taken him and where?'

'Scuffers,' he said. 'They've taken him in.'

'Scuffers!' my mother moaned. 'What are they?'

'Coppers!' I snarled at her. 'You've heard it before.' I jumped to my feet. 'What's he done, Darkie? There isn't much anybody can do on a Sunday afternoon in this dead place.'

'Nothin',' Darkie said. 'But they think he did it and that's as bad as if he did.'

'If he hasn't done it he's nothing to worry about,' Walter Higgins said. 'But what is it he's supposed to have done?'

Darkie watched him as if he were a fused bomb. 'Pinched your stuff.'

I gave a great snort. 'They're daft! Joe and me were with Robbo last night so he couldn't have done it.'

'It's where they found it,' Darkie said. 'Ain't anybody else knows the place 'cept me and Robbo, and I was in our house all night 'cos my Uncle Isaiah came from Birmingham.'

'And where did they find it?' Walter Higgins asked.

'Cleworth's,' Darkie said.

'Everybody in Benton knows the old mill,' Walter Higgins said. 'Used to play in it when I was a kid.'

Darkie was shaking his head. 'But Robbo and me, we've got a special place...'

I snorted again. 'I know it. I've been in it so why haven't the coppers taken me in?'

My mother moaned again. 'It's the boys you mix with. I always told you they'd land you in trouble.'

'I'm not in any trouble!' I told her.

'And there isn't anything wrong with young Robinson,' Walter Higgins said to her. 'The Robinsons are a decent family and he's a decent lad. I can't see him clouting Pop Burnett over the head.' He turned to Darkie. 'When did the police find the stuff? It isn't much more than an hour since I left them and they hadn't got a clue then.'

Darkie shook his head. 'Dunno, Mr Higgins. All I know is they came to our house about half an hour ago and asked where I was last night and then they went to Robbo's and took him and his pop away in a car. I came here to tell Dan 'cos he knows Robbo didn't do nothin'.'

'But what can Danny do?' my mother asked. 'I don't want him mixed up in this.'

'No, Mrs Rowley,' Darkie said, and then he stopped and I was sure that under the shining blackness of his skin he was blushing. 'No, Missus. Dan doesn't want to get mixed up in it.'

'I *am* mixed up in it!' I said. 'Robbo's a mate of mine.'

Darkie was still looking at my mother. 'Dan was there last night, Missus, and I thought he might think of somethin'. He's a clever lad at school.'

Lorna sniffed.

Then I saw Joe coming up the path, pushing his bike, and I made for the door.

'Here's Joe!' I said. 'Let's see if he can think of something.'

On the lawn in the front garden we told Joe all about it. At first he didn't listen very closely because Lorna was with us and he kept fidgeting, rubbing each dusty shoe on the back of the other leg and pressing his hair down. Then, before we'd finished, Jessie Watts came, in jeans and jumper, and pretty in a way you don't notice until you look hard.

'You know it wasn't Robbo,' Darkie said, ending the story. 'You was there with Robbo last night, but the scuffers has taken him in. T'aint fair.'

'It couldn't have been Robbo,' Joe said. 'He was there before us, wasn't he, Dan? But he couldn't have got all that stuff of your ... of Mr Higgins's away without us seeing him.'

'He wouldn't want to,' Darkie said. 'Robbo wouldn't pinch it. He isn't that kind. And he wouldn't have beat up old Pop either. Anyway, it must have been a big gang.'

Lorna snorted. 'A big gang! You don't think a big gang would steal a few pounds' worth of switches and things of my dad's? Big gangs rob banks and post offices.'

She was right. Joe was watching her and was thinking, and I knew that he thought she was right.

He nodded. 'It must have been somebody who knew the stuff was there and who would pinch anything. Like one of the men who work for Sadler's.'

And then I knew. 'Like Mugsy Jones,' I said.

Lorna sniffed. 'You lot blame Mugsy Jones for everything. It must be nice having somebody like him to blame for things. Very convenient, I must say.'

'It's just the sort of thing Mugsy would do,' I said. 'And he knew all that stuff was there because he saw it the other night.'

'You knew it was there too, didn't you?' she said in her sugary clever voice. 'And you were there last night. So why should it be Mugsy any more than you?'

''Cos Robbo hit him,' Darkie said, and when he saw us staring at him he went on, 'He said he'd get Robbo. Said he'd get all us coloured kids.'

Then I remembered. 'Robbo knocked him flat in our street! It's revenge, that's what!'

'But you can't prove it,' Lorna said.

Joe and I looked at her and Darkie looked at us. Jessie Watts was studying Walter Higgins's tulips.

'How could we make him confess?' I asked myself.

Lorna knew the way. 'Torture him,' she said. 'Like the Spanish Inquisition. There's three of you. You catch Mugsy and you take him somewhere quiet and you torture him until he confesses.'

'It's *cruel*!' Jessie said, and I liked her for saying it.

Lorna didn't. She sniffed and said, 'Have you got a better idea?'

Now we were all looking at Jessie and she blushed and said, 'You've got to trick him so that he confesses without knowing it. Then you'll be sure he did it.'

Lorna sighed. 'We know that, clever! But how?'

'Like this,' Jessie said so quietly that we leaned forward to listen to her. 'You could tell him something that would make him go back to Pop Burnett's hut if he'd done it and if he hadn't he wouldn't care so he wouldn't go.'

'Back to the scene of the crime,' I said. Jessie's quiet logic had started something throbbing in my mind.

'And what could they tell him?' Lorna asked her.

Jessie blushed again, embarrassed by our unwavering stares, but I knew that she had the answer. It was as if I was thinking with her and knew what she was going to say.

'They could tell him that whoever did it left a clue that the police are going to find tomorrow,' she said.

Lorna sniffed again but I exploded, 'That's it! It's a super idea!' Jessie turned away from the excited admiration in my eyes and I went on, 'We let it drop that the police are going over Pop's hut for finger-prints first thing in the morning. Then if Mugsy goes tonight we'll know he's guilty.'

'How will you know?' Lorna asked. 'How will you see him?'

'We'll be there,' I said. 'We'll be watching. There's plenty of places we can hide.'

'Your mother wouldn't let you go,' she said.

I grinned at her. 'Bet your father would.'

Joe was doubtful. 'I'll have to go and ask my mam. How about if we find Mugsy first and tell him?'

As it turned out it was easy to find Mugsy, but first we found Robbo. Joe, Darkie and I were passing the end of Cleworth Street when Darkie said, 'He's there! *Hey! Robbo!*'

Robbo was making slowly for the old mill, scuffing his feet and angrily kicking every stone as if he hated it. He turned and waited for us when we ran towards him.

'Where you been, boy?' he said to Darkie.

'For Dan,' Darkie said. 'I just had to tell somebody the

scuffers had taken you in and I thought Dan might think of something to help.'

Robbo looked at me, his eyes dark and resentful. 'Ain't going to need any help. It wouldn't do no good anyway.'

'Why wouldn't it?' I asked him.

''Cos all the scuffers in this town's *white*, boy. That's why.'

Although this came out of his confusion and bitterness it angered me.

'The coppers are O.K.,' I said. 'And don't you forget it.'

'Why did they let you go, Robbo?' Joe asked.

Robbo shrugged. 'Who knows about scuffers? They couldn't make out how I'd got all the stuff from Thorley, so they let me go until they find out.'

'They can't,' I said. 'You didn't do it.'

He shook his head. 'You want to hear that big detective, boy. "You help us, son, and we'll help you." That's how he talks. All he wants is for me to say I did it and then he can go home 'cos it's his day off.'

'We think Mugsy did it,' Darkie said. 'And we're goin' to prove it.'

There was no interest in Robbo's eyes as he looked at Darkie. 'Mugsy's white, boy,' he said.

'So what?' I said. 'You're talking like a big soft kid. You want to grow up.'

He turned to me and suddenly he smiled. 'O.K., boy. You tell me how Mugsy did it.'

'I'm not even sure he did do it, but I think he did. We're going to find out for sure by setting a trap. We're going to tell him that the coppers are going to the hut first thing tomorrow to look for finger-prints. If Mugsy did it he'll go there tonight to wipe them off and we'll be there watching.'

He thought about it, saying nothing for a time, and then Charlie McArthur came dashing round the corner.

He was the palest Negro I'd ever seen.

'You all right, Charlie?' I asked him.

He didn't hear me. 'Mugsy and that Snotty Smith are comin'!' he panted, looking at Robbo. 'They're after me and I think I'll find you at the old mill, so I run.'

'You're all right, boy,' Robbo said, his voice a deep rumble. 'Ain't nothin' to worry about. We'll do them.'

'We won't!' I said. 'This is our chance! Into the mill, quick!'

My urgency moved them. We streamed along the street and through the mill's doorway into the gloom and mustiness. That mill always smelled like the inside of a pyramid, as if it had been built for death. We huddled together a few feet from the door.

'I'll start talking as soon as we hear them coming,' I whispered. 'Then you say about the coppers looking for fingerprints in the morning, Robbo, and make it sound true.'

He studied me for a moment or two and then he nodded. 'O.K. I'll tell lies like you say, but they ain't true.'

I put a finger to my lips and we stood there listening. First we heard the throb of Mugsy's voice and then Snotty's squeaky laugh. As soon as I heard Mugsy's feet shuffling through the rubble I said in a loud voice, 'I knew they'd let you go, Robbo. You couldn't have done it because you were with me and Joe last night.'

I paused for a second to listen to the silence outside. Even the old mill was holding its breath. I went on, 'I bet they know who *did* do it. Did they tell you, Robbo?'

He shook his head and I grimaced at him. I nodded, I shook my fist, I mouthed urgencies at him, I begged him in every silent way I could think of to set the trap for Mugsy, but he only nodded.

It was Darkie who saved us. He said, 'The scuffers'll know for sure in the mornin', won't they, Robbo?'

This time Robbo spoke. 'That big detective's going to Pop's hut first thing tomorrow. He's taking some of them clever scuffers with him to look for finger-prints and he reckons they'll find plenty. Says he'll know tomorrow who beat old Pop up.'

'I'll bet it'll be somebody who's done something bad before,' Joe said. 'They'll have his finger-prints.'

'Like Mugsy Jones,' Charlie said, joining in the play, and I could have knocked him.

Instead I glared at him and we waited for the explosion of Mugsy's wrath, but outside there wasn't even a ripple in the silence. Cautiously I peeped round the doorframe and I saw Mugsy and Snotty hurrying away on tiptoe and leaning forward in their haste. I dodged back and leapt into the air.

'We've got 'em!' I sang, whispering.

Joe was peeping out. 'That proves they did it,' he said quietly. 'Bet they're on their way to Thorley right now.'

'No,' I said. 'Not in broad daylight. Mugsy's crafty. Snotty would be in a panic and he'd want to go, but Mugsy wouldn't. They'll go after dark and we've got to be there before them.'

They were all looking at me and I said, 'Somebody's got to be at Thorley. We've got to be sure Mugsy's the one.'

11 Confession

I could have gone to Thorley without my mother's permission, but that was never the way with us. So, even though she was now somebody called Mrs Higgins, I went to Walter Higgins's house and asked her. I told her about our plan to trap Mugsy and she said, 'I never heard anything like it!' which is one of the things grown-ups say when they need time to think.

'It's stupid,' Lorna said.

She'd been listening, her ears cocked to catch every word, and I swung on her and pointed at Jessie Watts.

'She thought of it!' I snarled. 'You only call it stupid because you didn't think of it yourself!'

'Jessie!' my mother said. 'What on earth gave you such an idea?'

Jessie's cheeks flamed and I felt so sorry for her I wanted to stroke her.

Walter Higgins said, 'A pretty nice idea, too, Jessie.'

We all stared at him, Jessie with gratitude, the rest of us with disbelief.

'Nice?' my mother said.

He gave her a nod. 'That Robinson lad's in trouble. It's always a nice idea to help somebody in trouble. You know, the Good Samaritan, Edith. Always liked that story.'

He went back to reading the Sunday paper and my mother said, 'You think he should go, Walter? It'll be dark. Is that what you want?'

He lowered his paper and said, 'It's what Danny wants.' He looked at me for a moment thoughtfully. 'How many of you are going?'

'Dunno. Robbo's sure and Joe's pretty sure. Darkie doesn't think his mother'll let him go and Charlie McArthur's too scared.'

My mother said, 'You know I never liked you going about with these Nigger boys, Danny.'

'The only Nigger boys are the ten in the nursery rhyme, or whatever it is,' Walter Higgins said to her, and then, to me, 'you're pretty sure the Jones boy knocked old Pop on the head?'

Lorna sniffed. 'They blame Mugsy Jones for everything. Just because he comes from a rotten home.'

'Give a dog a bad name,' my mother said.

Lorna smiled at her, forming a new alliance to defend Mugsy, and I got mad.

'It was Mugsy and Snotty Smith who broke into your place!' I said to Walter Higgins.

Lorna started to sing quietly and I flared at her, 'It was! I was there and I saw them. They broke in and pinched the money.'

'Why didn't you tell the police?' she asked sweetly. 'You never said it was them before.'

'Yes, Danny,' my mother said. 'Why have you been keeping this to yourself?'

It's wonderful how women stick together, thinking in ways too crafty for men.

I took a deep breath. ''Cos they told me if I snitched they'd say it was me, and they'd caught me doing it, and they were two on to one.'

'But I wouldn't have believed them, Danny,' my mother said.

I glared at Lorna. 'Some people would.'

She tossed her head and Walter Higgins said, 'Always thought it was the Jones boy. A real bad lot, that lad.' He picked up his paper again. 'I think he should go tonight, Edith.'

The telephone shrilled in the hall and he groaned. Lorna dashed towards the door but he stopped her with, 'Leave it, girl. It'll be for me.'

We sat without talking, listening to the deep rumble of his voice in the hall but unable to hear what he was saying, and then he came back.

'Fred Carr,' he said, and glanced at me. 'That's Joe's dad. Wants to know are you going tonight.'

'And what did you tell him?' my mother asked.

He sat down and grunted. 'I told him he was going. That all right with you, Edith?'

She sighed. 'It'll have to be, won't it?'

There was no hint in her voice of the relief I knew she felt at having had the decision taken for her, yet Walter Higgins must have known her almost as well as I did.

He said, 'Some things aren't easy to decide, Edith, particularly for a woman,' and he winked at me.

'But there's to be three of you, Dan,' he said. 'You don't tackle that Jones lad on your own.'

I nodded. 'Don't worry. I wouldn't go on my own. It's too dark round Thorley.'

'You'd best take my flashlight,' he said, 'but don't lose it. It's what I use when I'm working in lofts.'

'You never lent it to me!' Lorna said, her glare scorching him.

She dashed out of the room and Jessie, too embarrassed to live with us, slipped after her. A moment later I heard them in the garden.

'Now what was all that?' Walter Higgins said.

'You've got to be careful with two children,' my mother said. 'They get so jealous of one another.'

'Jealous!' I said. 'You won't see me getting jealous of *her*!'

'That's enough, my lad,' my mother said. 'You're getting a sight too uppity these days.'

'Not half as uppity as Lorna,' Walter Higgins said. 'I don't know where she gets it from. It can't be little Jessie Watts.'

'She doesn't get it from anybody,' my mother said. 'It's the way things are. She wants to be handled carefully. And Jessie Watts is a very nice girl. It's just a pity she's so quiet.'

'She's none the worse for that,' Walter Higgins said. 'She may be quiet, but there's plenty going on inside that head of hers.' He stood up. 'I'll get that flashlight, lad, and then you'll be ready when Joe comes.'

So we went to Thorley, Robbo, Joe and I, three of us, so excited that the road seemed twice as long as usual, and by the time we got there the certainty was heavy inside me that Mugsy would never come. It was almost dark and night was infiltrating the little hills of Thorley. The half-built bungalows stood like ruins in some lost land.

'Where we going to hide?' Joe whispered.

Across the road from Pop's hut there was a ditch and leaning over it from the other side a clump of elderberry bushes.

I pointed at them. 'In there.'

We jumped the ditch and crawled into the bushes, scattering some roosting birds that flew out complaining. Robbo yelped at the sudden clatter and my heart hammered my ribs. I swung on him and saw his eyes, like two beacons in the gloom.

'Shurrup!' I hissed at him.

'I'm scared, boy,' he said.

There was a hollow, lined with leaves, in the middle of the bushes and we nestled there and looked through the pattern of foliage at Pop's white hut, the only thing still visible to us in the darkness.

'If they come we'll see them,' I said to convince myself.

'You got eyes like a cat?' Robbo whispered. 'Soon you won't see nothin'.'

I patted Walter Higgins's flashlight. 'You wait. This thing's as good as a searchlight.'

We waited for a long time. Night took over so completely that we could no longer see the hut or the road or each other. A cold breeze blew through the bushes and stiffened us, and every movement we made was an upheaval in that cramped hollow. I saw the flicker of stars through the leaves, and Robbo's eyes, which seemed to have a light of their own.

'They ain't comin',' he said, 'and I wanna go home.'

'You're staying here!' I whispered furiously. 'It's because of you we're doing this.'

'It wasn't my idea,' he said. 'I'd rather be in our house watchin' telly.'

'Wouldn't we all!' Joe said.

We crouched for another half-hour, all the time wondering what foolishness had once made the plan seem good. I blamed Jessie Watts for suggesting it and myself for thinking that a girl's idea could be of any use. Robbo cautiously stretched his legs, groaning quietly, and I said savagely, 'It's a dead loss! Let's clear off!'

I had started to crawl out of the bushes when Joe grabbed my ankle and whispered, 'Listen!'

I froze, like a startled rabbit, on all fours, and I listened to footsteps shuffling stealthily along the road. I wriggled back until I could look at the place in the darkness where the hut was, and now the footsteps were only a few yards away and I heard somebody whisper, 'There it is!'

Robbo was trembling so hard beside me that he was shaking the bushes. We heard no more whispering and we saw nothing, although I thought that for a moment a shape, like a tree, stood where no tree had been before, but I blinked and it was no longer there.

I stared until my eyes ached and listened to the blood surging through my ears, and then I heard a sharp alien sound, the clink of metal on metal, and Robbo moaned softly.

'They're at the door!' Joe whispered.

There was a long screech like a nail being drawn slowly out of wood and I said, 'They're inside!'

I aimed the flashlight and pressed the switch. The beam split the darkness round the hut and trapped Snotty Smith in the open doorway, blinking and twitching his nose like a cornered rat. Before he could move he was hurled aside and Mugsy stood there for a second, desperate and defiant, glaring at the light. He leapt away from the hut and went rushing up into the little hills while we fought to find a way out of the tangle of branches. I was first out and I leapt across the ditch and, as I landed, I heard a squelch and turned the light on Joe, up to his knees in mud but scrambling out. Robbo went past me so smoothly that he scarcely seemed to touch the ground, and by the time I'd helped Joe up the bank he had gone.

I sent the flashlight beam exploring into the hills and it soon found Snotty teetering along and trying to regain the firm safety of the road.

'Get him!' I shouted.

Joe and I started together, but long before we could reach Snotty we saw Robbo leap like a panther out of the blackness and bring him down. When we got to them Snotty was on his back with Robbo sitting on his chest and rumbling softly to him, 'I'm gonna beat your face in, boy.'

Snotty looked up at me and pleaded, 'Don't let him! Pull him off!'

'I'm gonna kick your teeth in!' Robbo said.

'And we'll help you,' I said.

Snotty was a wreck. He had neither courage nor character and the cunning he used in all other situations was no help to him in this one. Desperation made him heave and struggle but Robbo was too agile for him.

I remembered Lorna and I said, 'We'll torture him till he confesses.'

'Best if I just kick his teeth in,' Robbo said.

'*No!*' Snotty screamed. 'I'll snitch!'

'O.K.,' I said. 'Who was it beat up Pop and pinched all the stuff out of the hut?'

Snotty gulped in a deep breath. 'It was Mugsy knocked him out. He'll kill me if he finds out, but he did it with a lump of wood he picked up outside the hut. Him and me, we carried all the stuff back and we hid it in the old mill. I didn't want to but Mugsy made me. He said he was goin' to fix you proper.'

'Them scuffers think I did it,' Robbo said.

'And it was you and Mugsy broke into Walter Higgins's place, wasn't it?' I asked. 'And you pinched the money.'

Snotty tried to nod. 'Mugsy only gave me ten bob and he kept the rest for himself and spent it.'

Beside me in the darkness Joe let out a long sigh. 'That's about it. Flippin' heck! He's told us the lot!'

'And a fat lot of good it is,' I said.

Robbo banged Snotty's head on the ground. 'It's good for you, ain't it, boy? You got it off your chest, didn't you?'

'It's not much good for us,' I said. 'It'd only be any good if he'd told it to the coppers.'

'I'll tell them!' Snotty said, and I knew he was a liar.

'You already told us,' somebody said.

I whirled round and Joe jumped straight over Snotty. The detective was there, Detective Sergeant Garside, looking bigger than ever. He clicked on the flashlight in his fist and added its beam to mine.

'Let him get up, son,' he said to Robbo. 'I'll take over from here.'

Robbo swung smoothly to his feet and backed away and Snotty scrambled up groaning.

'You won't tell my old man, will you, sir?' he wheedled. 'He'll kill me.'

'I won't tell him,' the detective said. 'But you're going to. That's where I'm taking you now – to your father so you can tell him all about it. If he kills you it'll save the Jones boy a job.'

Snotty sobbed. 'He will too. Mugsy'll kill me.'

'Not where he'll be going,' the detective said.

A thought was surfacing in my brain and I said, 'How did you know we were here?'

He chuckled and sounded unexpectedly like any other man. 'Information received, son.'

I snorted. 'I bet it was Walter Higgins, and he phoned you!'

'You may be right. Whoever it was he did a pretty good job.' He looked at me for a time, thinking. 'You and me both make the same mistakes, son. We jump to conclusions about people too quick, don't we?'

I didn't know, and I was still wondering about it when a car came nosing along the road, its headlights thrusting the shadows of the little hills far across the country. It stopped and a copper got out, and it was the copper who'd caught me smashing gaslamps.

'Another car's on its way, Sarge,' he said.

The detective nodded. 'You run these lads home, will you?' He put his big hand on Snotty's shoulder. 'I'll stay here with Mr Moriarty and take him home in the other car.'

Snotty moaned and the constable said, 'O.K., you lads. Jump in.'

We sat together in the back, Robbo in the middle,

trembling with triumph. Suddenly I was weak and tired.

Robbo said, 'For ages I been wantin' to have a ride in one of these, but not if it was takin' me in. I wanted to ride in one when the blue flasher was going on top of it.'

There was the click of a switch and the copper said, 'O.K., son. You've got your wish. But don't you tell the sergeant. He'd have the pants off me.'

12 Rogue

School next day and Wally Sinton making one of his speeches in the hall after prayers; a speech about our Saturday-morning match against Cronton. There was no ring of triumph in his voice, but there was a quiet satisfaction expressed in what he said. At the end of the speech he made the team stand up while the school applauded us. I could see Mugsy at the back, a derisive grin on his face.

It was the first time I'd seen Mugsy that morning. Joe and Robbo and Darkie and I had looked for him before the whistle, but we hadn't found him because Wally Sinton had had him in his room. I don't know what changes we'd expected to see in him; perhaps a new fear, a strange submissiveness. Now he was with us in the hall, more rebellious than ever, and showing by the thunder of his hands his scorn for all authority.

Across the hall Jessie Watts was clapping, her eyes only on me. It was funny how in a couple of days I'd grown shy of that girl. She was the first girl who'd ever looked at me in a personal way, as if we had some secret understanding. Perhaps we had. I know that because of her I'd started to water down my hair and brush my teeth without being told to.

It was break when we saw Mugsy. Joe, Robbo, Darkie and I kept together, all of us excited, each of us made nervous by the certainty that Mugsy was still a danger. First we found Wilf Brady, afraid of us yet hating us as only a kid can hate.

'You lot better watch it!' he growled at us.

'Why?' I said. 'What'll you do?'

'Not me. I'm not big enough, but Mugsy is and he hasn't half got it in for you gang.'

I grinned. 'What did we do to Mugsy?'

He grunted. 'As if you didn't know! The coppers had him nearly all last night. They went to Snotty's first and then ...'

'Haven't seen Snotty today,' Joe said.

Wilf Brady shook his head. 'You aren't the only one. He's stayed away and I don't blame him. Mugsy knows it was him snitched to the coppers and Mugsy'll do him.'

'Mugsy won't be doin' anybody,' Robbo rumbled.

'Won't he? You don't know what he's like. He's a mate o' mine but he scares me and I'm keepin' away from him. His dad clouted him last night and then he tried to clout his dad and his dad half killed him. You know Mugsy's dad? He's a massive chap, as big as one of them dinosaurs, and I wouldn't like him to clout me. The coppers said that Mugsy was sure to be put away this time and his dad said a good thing too.'

'He's comin'!' Darkie Bates whispered.

We turned round and there was Mugsy, a tousled gorilla, shuffling towards us, the derisive grin still on his face and in his eyes a scorn for all conformers, for the obedient and the good.

'How's crime?' he said, and then, before any of us could speak, 'I don't like kids who snitch to teachers and coppers.'

'So what?' I said, not afraid of him yet not understanding him. The trouble with Mugsy was that nobody understood him, nobody talked in a language that was clear to him.

'You think it's kids like me what cause all the trouble,' he said. 'You're wrong. It's teachers and coppers and the kids who snitch to them.' He looked straight at Robbo. 'I can't do nothin' about teachers and coppers yet, but I can do plenty about kids. It'll be a week or two before my case comes up. See you in Borstal.'

He swung round and left us and we were silent.

Wilf Brady whispered. 'See what I mean? I wouldn't be one of you lot. He's a nut case.'

I was suddenly angry and he was the only one I could be angry with.

'You'd best clear off!' I snarled at him. 'He's your mate, isn't he?'

He stared at me, puzzled, and then he turned and ran, leaving me with my anger unquenched.

I didn't see Mugsy again at school that day. I went home on my own after four o'clock. Jessie Watts and Lorna were hanging about outside school, but I dodged them and I was in the house and up in my room waiting, with my hands washed, for tea before Lorna came home.

Tea was a quiet meal. Lorna seemed to be trying different tactics, quietly accepting my mother and me as if we'd been in the family for years. But I knew we hadn't and I was nervous of the explosion that was always dormant in her. She ignored her father so much that I felt sorry for him, while there was a sweetness in her voice when she spoke to my mother that made me feel sick.

I was waiting for the others to reach the cake stage when she looked across the table at me and said, 'Jessie's coming tonight.'

I could feel the blush starting in my neck, but I fought it down.

'So what?' I said.

'So she wants to go out with you,' she said.

My face flamed and she laughed. Walter Higgins chuckled, but I knew he was only trying to keep in with her.

'Shurrup!' I threw at her.

She tossed her head. 'Boys! They're uncouth!'

I was wondering what that meant when my mother said, 'Jessie's a nice girl.'

'She's daft!' I said. 'All girls are daft!'

'That's enough of that, my lad,' my mother said, 'and don't speak with your mouth full.'

I glared at her, but she and Lorna were smiling at each other in the smug way women have.

'So you'll be staying in, Dan?' Walter Higgins said.

'Not on your life!' I said. 'I'm off out.'

'I was wondering if you'd anything special on tonight,' he said.

I nodded and he said, 'Joe coming?'

'We're going to see Pop,' I told him. 'He's due out of hospital today and we thought we'd go and see him.'

'"Pop"?' my mother said. '*Mister* Burnett's old enough to be your grandfather.' Then she looked at Walter Higgins but said to me, 'And I've told you I don't like you going to Gaskin Street.'

'You don't mind me going?' he said to her. 'Wouldn't be a bad idea if you came with me, Edith. Must be a long time since you had a word with Pop Burnett.'

She said nothing and he turned to me. 'Have you time to come out with me first? Won't take half an hour.'

I was so sorry for him that I never thought of refusing or of asking him where we were going. I jumped up, my mouth still full of cake, and I said, 'We'd best get going then. Joe won't be long and if I'm out he'll have to talk to *girls*.'

I glared at Lorna, but she only smiled at my mother.

We went in Walter Higgins's car and I scarcely noticed where we were going because I was watching him drive, trying to learn about the gears and clutch ready for when I was old enough to drive. So in no time at all we were pulling up in one of Benton's duller streets, and it was a few seconds before I realised that it was our old street and that we'd stopped in front of our old house. The sun was still shining, yet it had become a meaner, shabbier sun.

I looked straight at Walter Higgins. 'What's the idea?'

'Come on,' he said, climbing out of the car.

He opened our front door with a key my mother must have given him and I followed him into the dark passage we'd always called a hall. None of the weak sunshine found its way into this house, through the tiny windows my mother had spent so much time cleaning. The air was stale, as if it had been breathed too often. Everywhere there was dinginess and I was ashamed.

'Why've you brought me here?' I growled at Walter Higgins without looking at him.

He walked into the kitchen. 'Because you ought to have some say about things. Your mother's going to sell up. What do you think?'

I shrugged. 'Doesn't matter, does it?'

'It matters a lot. If there's anything you want to keep it'll be kept. What about it?'

I glanced round at the old furniture which had in so short a time become strange and disagreeable to me. I said, 'Sell the lot,' and I felt a traitor.

'Nothing you want to keep?'

I shook my head and he must have understood because he said, 'Sometimes we've all got to be ruthless. No amount of wishing'll bring back what's gone and the best thing's to make a fresh start.'

I didn't want his sympathy. I was still looking at the old furniture and the jaded ornaments, and thinking how Lorna's sarcasm would be spilled over anything we took from this house to the brightness of Walter Higgins's.

'No point in keeping any of it,' I said. 'I suppose we're going on living at your house?'

He nodded slowly. 'I suppose.'

We went back in the car, neither of us saying a word, and I even forgot to watch him driving. When we pulled up outside his house my mother and Lorna were on the front lawn with Joe, his hair watered down and his face scrubbed. He nodded to me.

'Come on,' I said to him. 'Let's go see old Pop.'

We walked through the new property that straggled round the edge of Benton. For some years people had been building their houses in the pleasant country outside Benton so that the town was like one of those fairy rings you sometimes find in a meadow; dead in the middle but living and spreading outwards.

Then Joe and I cut across to Gaskin Street and found old Pop sitting on a wooden chair in a patch of sunlight which was falling on to the footpath near to his front door.

' 'Lo, you lads!' he said. 'Where are you off to?' He was shrunken and pale and the youth his eyes had always retained had now vanished. His hair and beard were of a brighter whiteness, bleached no doubt in the hospital. Yet his spirit was undamaged.

'Are you better, Mr Burnett?' I asked.

He gave a nod. 'Them doctors and nurses didn't think so but I knew that my own house with Mrs Yates keeping an eye on me would get me better quicker than they could.' He snorted. 'Folk die in hospital.'

'Mr Higgins is coming to see you, Pop,' Joe said.

'Knew he would. A good lad, is Walter.' He glanced at me, screwing up his papery eyelids against the sun. 'A fine footballer he was, too. And you aren't so bad yourself, Dan Rowley. That was a grand goal you scored, Saturday, and I liked the way you took it. I never saw a better goal than that.'

I started to blush and shuffle and I said, 'Joe's was as good.'

He nodded. 'Ay, but it's easier for Joe. He's a better

footballer. I mind Walter Sinton when he was a boy and Joe's like him. But you had to work for your goal, lad, and you took it well. Keep on living that way and you'll never go far wrong. Know what I mean?'

I shook my head and he looked at me.

'You've got to have a goal in life and you've got to work for it. That's what I mean.' He cleared the phlegm out of his throat. 'That's what's wrong with Mugsy Jones. He hasn't got a goal in life. Pity he never plays football. Fancy him hittin' me over the head! I've known that lad since he was a baby.'

'I don't suppose he meant to hurt you, Pop,' Joe said.

'Ay, but he did, Joe. That's just the point. His dad brought him to say he was sorry, but I wouldn't let him 'cos he wasn't. You've got to feel sorry and he didn't. He thinks it's everybody's fault but his. Puts me in mind of an elephant.'

I laughed. I couldn't help it. 'An elephant!'

'Ay. One o' them rogue elephants the herd'd thrown out. Mugsy's a rogue and everybody's thrown him out.' Pop looked at the dead ash in his pipe. 'Saw him a few minutes before you lads came. He was going that way.' He nodded towards the end of the street where the cindery desert lay. 'That way. He crossed over to the other side so's he wouldn't have to pass close by me and there was a funny look on his face. Shifty.' He spat. 'Furtive. That's the word. He needs watchin'. No tellin' what he'll get up to before his case comes up. After that I don't think anybody'll need to watch him for a year or two.'

'He may have gone to the old mill,' I said.

Pop nodded. 'Cleworth's. That's what I was thinkin'. That's where some of them coloured boys hang about and Mugsy doesn't like them. He's got it in for them. He doesn't like anybody, but he fair hates them coloured boys.'

'We'll go and have a look,' Joe said, 'and we'll come back and let you know, Pop.'

We left him there, sitting in the evening sun, which shone through his transparent skin and lit up his white hair like a halo.

13 Cocoa for Everybody

Once we were on the cindery desert Joe and I almost
forgot Mugsy. We threw stones into the scummy pools
and watched the slime spatter the ground. It's the sort of
game lads can play for a long time and we played it until
Joe paused, his stone-primed hand raised above his head.

'Hear that?' he asked.

I'd heard something, some foreign sound which was
no part of the normal Benton rumble. I nodded and we
made for the wall, climbed it and sat on top of it.
Cleworth Street was empty. The rubble and the brambles
and the willowherb were still there, but there was nobody to disturb them, no voice to bring life to that dead
street.

'What d'you reckon it was?' Joe whispered.

Then we heard another sound, a thud, as if a box or a
body had been dumped on to a hollow floor.

'Flippin' heck!' Joe said, and I was leaping after him
and chasing him across the street towards the mill.

We dashed through the empty doorway and stopped
while our eyes adjusted to the gloom. Now I could hear
more sounds and I knew them to be grunts and curses
and the kicking of feet on a floor. Although my eyes
could still not penetrate the shadows, I ran for the old
stairs, tearing through the cobwebs that clutched softly
at my face. I leapt up the stairs on to the swaying floor
and I saw Mugsy Jones astride another boy, a boy with
crinkly Negro hair, and holding above his face a small

bright knife. The Negro boy's long fingers were wrapped round Mugsy's wrist and he was wrestling with Mugsy's arm to keep the knife away. But I could see his shoulder sagging and I heard Mugsy pant, 'I'm gonna do you! I'm gonna make you so's you won't know yourself, Nigger!'

The whole weight of his heavy body pressed the knife down and the Negro boy gasped and sobbed, and I took a running kick at Mugsy's straining fist and Mugsy shrieked and the knife went spinning into one of the mill's dark recesses.

As Mugsy turned on me, Joe went past me like a whirlwind and his shoulder took Mugsy in the stomach and doubled him up. Mugsy toppled over the edge of the wooden floor on to the old bricks ten feet below and, although we listened hard, we heard no sound from him.

The Negro boy was scrambling to his feet, his eyes still telling of his fear.

'I'm glad you kids come,' he said.

It was Darkie Bates, shooting white-eyed glances into the farthest shadows.

'Where'd that Mugsy Jones go?' he asked.

I stepped unwillingly to the edge of the floor and looked down. Beside me Joe said, 'Flippin' heck! I killed him, Dan!'

Mugsy was face down on the brick floor, an immense and motionless sprawl.

'You think they'll say it was murder, Dan?' Joe asked me in a frightened whisper. 'Or that other thing ... manslaughter? I wasn't meaning to slaughter anybody.'

Then somebody came running in through the bright doorway and paused while his eyes found us in the shadows.

'It's Robbo!' Darkie sang out. 'I'm O.K., Robbo! Mugsy was gonna carve me up but these kids stopped him!'

Robbo stalked silently towards Mugsy and Mugsy suddenly leapt up and away from him.

Darkie chuckled. 'That Mugsy Jones! He was only foolin' all the time.'

But Mugsy wasn't fooling now. He was afraid of the vengeance steadily approaching him. He sobbed, glanced round and, in an explosive dash, made for the door. As I ran down the stairs I saw him framed in the light for an instant, his whole terrified being concentrated on escape. We ran outside after him, Darkie yelping, and there was Walter Higgins catching Robbo by the arm and stopping him, and my mother turning to watch Mugsy's flight.

'He's terrified,' she said.

Walter Higgins was looking into Robbo's deep eyes. 'You don't want his blood as well, do you?' he said.

Robbo shook his head. 'No, sir.'

'Then let him go,' Walter Higgins said. 'You've frightened the life out of him. You don't have to worry about him any more.'

'I'm sorry for him,' my mother said. 'It's time somebody took a needle to his trousers.'

Walter Higgins saw me watching him and he nodded.

'We came to see old Pop. Your mother brought him some flowers out of the front garden. He told us you'd come here after Mugsy so we came in the car. It's just round the corner.'

Joe said, 'Think I'd best be gettin' home, Dan.'

'We'll take you in the car, Joe,' Walter Higgins said. 'You can have a cup of cocoa with Danny before you set out on your bike.'

He started to turn away but I hadn't done with him yet.

'What about them?' I said, pointing at Robbo and Darkie, who was grinning shyly. 'They drink cocoa too.'

He stopped and gave me a quick look and then he

chuckled. 'So do I. Let's all go and have a cup of cocoa, shall we, Edith?'

My mother's eyes opened wider, but he took her arm and said, 'Cocoa for everybody!'

more TOPLINERS for your enjoyment

by E. W. HILDICK
Birdy in Amsterdam
The canals of Amsterdam lead Birdy into deep water.

by ROY WILSON
First Season
Life is tough for Danny before he makes the big time in football.

by DIANNE DOUBTFIRE
Escape on Monday
Veronica and her mother begin to understand each other after a dramatic conflict over Veronica's boy friend, Terry.

Edited by AIDAN CHAMBERS
I Want to Get Out
An anthology of prose and poetry by teenage writers.

by CHRISTOPHER LEACH
Decision for Katie
Katie finds that looking after Graham involves more than she imagined.

by PAUL ZINDEL
The Pigman
Life is simple for a generous old man until he meets two American teenagers.

Compiled by AIDAN and NANCY CHAMBERS
World Zero Minus: An S. F. Anthology
An exciting collection of science-fiction stories.

TOPLINERS published by Macmillan

more TOPLINERS for your enjoyment

by AIDAN CHAMBERS

Ghosts 2

Follows *Ghosts* with more spine-chilling stories of the super-natural.

by HONOR ARUNDEL

The Girl in the Opposite Bed

Jane hates being in hospital but by the time she goes home she knows much more about people – herself as well as others.

by INGER BRATTSTROM

Since That Party

Odd-man-out Nicholas, who adores popular Stella from afar, gives a birthday party ... with unforeseeable consequences.

Compiled by JOHN L. FOSTER

That's Love

Twelve stories which speak of love – its hopes and fears, joys and anguish.

by CHRISTINE DICKENSON

Siege at Robins Hill

Awkward relatives, the Children's Department, even the Police, cannot break Janice's resolve to keep her orphaned family together.

and many other titles – send to the publishers for a complete list.

The editor of Topliners is always pleased to hear what readers think of the books and to receive ideas for new titles. If you want to write to him please address your letter to: The Editor, Topliners, Macmillan, Houndmills, Basingstoke, Hampshire RG21 2XS. All letters received will be answered.

TOPLINERS published by Macmillan